September's menu
BARONESSA GELATERIA
in Boston's North End

In addition to our regular flavors of gelato, this month we are featuring:

- **Imported full-bodied espresso**

  With his dark eyes, swarthy skin and sensuous mouth, Ashraf ibn-Saalem, Prince of Zhamyr, was one gorgeous sheikh. Rich, smart, worldly, sexy…and virile. Just the man to father Karen Rawlins's baby and give her child a heritage.

- **Chocolate Kisses**

  To seal their bargain, Ash insisted on a kiss. A rock-my-world kiss that left Karen's lips swollen, hot and wet. She knew his insistence on making a baby the conventional way would certainly be fun…but would it be wise?

- **Hot quick bread with vanilla ice cream**

  Despite a rushed wedding, their baby-making was anything but. The sheikh's slow exploration of her body was sweet torture. His hands and tongue ignited a trail of heat over her sensitive skin that left her parched as a desert and thirsty for more. But that wasn't part of the plan.…

Buon appetito!

Dear Reader,

Welcome to another stellar month of stories from Silhouette Desire. We kick things off with our DYNASTIES: THE BARONES series as Kristi Gold brings us *Expecting the Sheikh's Baby* in which—yes, you guessed it!—a certain long-lost Barone cousin finds herself expecting a very special delivery.

Also this month: The fabulous Peggy Moreland launches a brand-new series with THE TANNERS OF TEXAS, about *Five Brothers and a Baby,* which will give you the giddy-up you've been craving. The wonderful Brenda Jackson is back with another story about her Westmoreland family. *A Little Dare* is full of many big surprises…including a wonderful secret-child story line. And *Sleeping with the Boss* by Maureen Child will have you on the edge of your seat—or boardroom table, whatever the case may be.

KING OF HEARTS, a new miniseries by Katherine Garbera, launches with *In Bed with Beauty*. The series focuses on an angel with some crooked wings who must do a lot of matchmaking in order to secure his entrance through the pearly gates. And Laura Wright is back with *Ruling Passions,* a very sensual royal-themed tale.

So, get ready for some scintillating storytelling as you settle in for six wonderful novels. And next month, watch for Diana Palmer's *Man in Control*.

More passion to you!

Melissa Jeglinski

Melissa Jeglinski
Senior Editor, Silhouette Desire

Expecting the Sheikh's Baby

KRISTI GOLD

Published by Silhouette Books
America's Publisher of Contemporary Romance

Special thanks and acknowledgment are given to
Kristi Gold for her contribution to the
DYNASTIES: THE BARONES series.

Acknowledgments

Special thanks to former Bostonite and honorary Texan Sandy Blair for her incredible information and wonderful insight.

SILHOUETTE BOOKS

ISBN 0-373-76531-2

EXPECTING THE SHEIKH'S BABY

This edition published by arrangement with Harlequin Books S.A.

Visit Silhouette at www.eHarlequin.com

Printed in U.S.A.

Books by Kristi Gold

Silhouette Desire

Cowboy for Keeps #1308
Doctor for Keeps #1320
His Sheltering Arms #1350
Her Ardent Sheikh #1358
**Dr. Dangerous* #1415
**Dr. Desirable* #1421
**Dr. Destiny* #1427
His E-Mail Order Wife #1454
The Sheikh's Bidding #1485
**Renegade Millionaire* #1497
Marooned with a Millionaire #1517
Expecting the Sheikh's Baby #1531

*Marrying an M.D.

KRISTI GOLD

has always believed that love has remarkable healing powers and feels very fortunate to be able to weave stories of romance and commitment. As a bestselling author and a Romance Writers of America RITA® Award finalist, she's learned that although accolades are wonderful, the most cherished rewards come from the most unexpected places, namely from personal stories shared by readers. Kristi resides on a ranch in Central Texas with her husband and three children, along with various and sundry livestock. She loves to hear from readers and can be contacted at KGOLDAUTHOR@aol.com or P.O. Box 11292, Robinson, TX 76716.

DYNASTIES: THE BARONES

Meet the Barones of Boston—
an elite clan caught in a web of danger,
deceit...and desire!

Who's Who in
EXPECTING THE SHEIKH'S BABY

Ashraf ibn-Saalem—After a painful betrayal, this Arabian sheikh has put his heart on ice, but not his libido. His shrewd, dark eyes appreciate women, but his hardened heart vows never to love again. But there is one thing he wants—a child.

Karen Rawlins—Some say this long-lost Barone cousin is unbendable, stubborn, unyielding. Karen says she's her own woman. At thirty-one, she hears her biological clock ticking and sees a child of her own in her nightly dreams. But she'd just as soon subtract the husband from the baby-making equation.

Maria Barone—More than anyone, she knows that no matter what you want, you can't run away from what fate has in store....

Prologue

The man could be her father, but that was impossible.

Her father was dead.

Karen Rawlins touched her trembling fingertips to the photograph of Paul Barone included in the Boston newspaper along with a story covering the Barone family's latest reunion. The article also reported the tale of the unsolved mystery from years ago surrounding the abduction of Paul's twin brother, Luke, serving as confirmation of what Karen had recently learned from the yellowed pages of her grandmother's diary—her loving grandparents had lived a lie for over half a century.

Karen sat in the only home she had known, deep in the heart of Montana, while too many unanswered questions haunted her as keenly as her memories. Had her father known about the journal Karen had found among her grandmother's belongings? Had he learned of the deception before his untimely death? Had he known that he had been born to a wealthy Massachusetts family only to be kidnapped by the woman he had always considered his mother, and that his name was not Timothy Rawlins but Luke Barone?

Karen tossed the newspaper aside knowing she would never have all the answers she craved. Everyone who could fill in the blanks was gone. Her grandparents had died only months apart two years before in peaceful slumber, and her parents had been killed in a devastating car crash a year ago.

Dealing with the overwhelming loss and this new insight into her family tree might have been easier if Karen hadn't ended her engagement to Carl. But that had been a blessing. She preferred to live her life alone as long as she could live her life as she wanted. That had not been Carl's intent. Carl's intent had involved control. He'd wanted a wife who would hang her life on his whims, not a woman with dreams and opinions and career goals. She refused to mourn that ending.

Karen wrapped her hands around a mug of coffee, trying to absorb some warmth, though the July weather outside was warm and wonderful. Still she felt chilled to the marrow, even in the comfortable kitchen that smelled of cinnamon and radiated kindness, an ideal depiction of home and hearth. She also felt utterly alone.

Needless to say, it had not been a banner year for Karen Rawlins. It then occurred to her that she had no reason to stay in Silver Valley. The single-stoplight town had nothing to offer but bittersweet recollections and the realization that much of what she'd believed about her family, her legacy, was false—except for the fact that her parents and grandparents had loved her without reservation.

Perhaps Boston held more opportunities. Exciting opportunities. A place to regroup and grow. Karen decided then and there to seek out the Barones, to tell Paul what details she knew about his missing brother with the hope that the family would welcome her with open arms and open minds. She would find a good job and maybe one day establish her own interior design business. She would make a good life for herself. A new life. And in order to fill the empty space in her soul, Karen would attempt to have a child, someone to love her without conditions.

No, it had not been a banner year for Karen Rawlins, but it could be—would be—from this point forward. She would simply have to make it happen, and she would achieve all of her goals without the interference of a man.

One

Oh, heck, not him again.

From behind the marble counter of the Barone family's famed Baronessa Gelateria, Karen Rawlins knocked her elbow on the edge of the cash register and stifled a yelp that would surely drown out the rendition of ''Santa Lucia'' filtering from the overhead speakers. She also bit back a litany of mild curses directed at the lone man seated in the corner booth next to the windows. A man who stood out like a searchlight among the Barone family Italian ice-cream shop's simple, traditional decor.

Karen prided herself on having a designer's eye and this particular male was designed to perfection. His exotic good looks presented the perfect portrait of the consummate dark, mysterious stranger.

But Sheikh Ashraf Saalem was no stranger to Karen. She'd met him last month during the welcoming party given in her honor by the Barones. Yes, he had been somewhat charming, maybe even slightly charismatic—okay, more than slightly—but much too confident for Karen's comfort. As far as she was concerned, overt confidence denoted control. She didn't care for controlling men, even if they could give a woman the shakes with only a sultry look, and he'd given her plenty of those the last time she'd been in his company. She also hadn't been able to forget what else he had given her that night.

A kiss.

An earth-tilting, knock-me-over, make-me-tremble kiss. A kiss she hadn't been able to ignore.

But she had to ignore it, ignore him, especially now. Ignore his occasional glances, his eyes as dark as Baronessa's popular espresso. Not an easy task even though he had exchanged his traditional Arabian clothing for professional corporate attire—a beige silk suit and a turtleneck pullover as black as his silky thick hair. He looked like any businessman taking a break from the fast-paced corporate world of finance, yet he still exuded an authoritative aura. But he wasn't just any man, a fact that had become all too apparent from the moment Karen had met him—and kissed him.

After one more furtive glance, Karen went back to straightening the sundae bowls lined up beneath the counter. She had a job to do, a nice job working in the gelateria alongside her wonderful cousin, Maria. Almost a month ago, she'd been lovingly welcomed by her new family, had accepted the assistant manager position and in turn gained a whole slew of relatives as well as a nice apartment that had once belonged to her other cousin Gina. Now that her life was back on track, she certainly didn't have the time or desire to be distracted by a man, even if he happened to be a charismatic prince.

As if her will had left the building without her, Karen

stole another quick glance. How could she possibly overlook his presence since the shop was practically deserted? No surprise the place was empty considering the post-lunch hour and that the earlier September deluge had now ended. Those who had taken refuge from the elements had made their way back into the Boston streets to resume their midafternoon activities.

Everyone except the sheikh. He was the only patron aside from another couple sequestered in the opposing corner booth, holding hands and talking in whispers while their gelato turned to fruity soup. What a waste of good ice cream, Karen thought. What a display of ridiculous sentimentality.

Karen mentally scolded herself for her cynical attitude. Who could say this particular couple wouldn't find forever happiness? Just because she had decided she wouldn't drape her dreams on a life partner didn't mean others couldn't find that proverbial soul mate.

"I see you have a visitor."

Karen's gaze snapped from the love duo to Maria's subtle smile and mischievous wide brown eyes. "Why didn't you tell me he'd come in?" She honestly hadn't meant to sound so irritable, but watching the young couple moon over each other had prompted Karen's less-than-jovial mood. So had Ashraf ibn-Saalem's surprise appearance.

"You were down in the basement when he arrived," Maria said. "And I didn't realize you would be so interested."

"I'm not." Karen slapped a rag across a counter that didn't need cleaning, working it over with a vengeance. "As far as I'm concerned, he's just another customer having his coffee."

Maria moved to Karen's side and sent a not-so-discreet

glance in the sheikh's direction. ''My guess is he didn't come in here to escape the rain or to have coffee or gelato.'' She leaned closer to Karen and said in a whisper, ''Considering the look he keeps giving you, I do believe he could be here for a different kind of dessert, if you know what I mean.''

Karen knew exactly what Maria had meant, and she wasn't about to be the sheikh's sweet, now or ever. Turning her back to the dining room, she leaned against the counter and shot a quick glance over her shoulder. ''He's not giving me any kind of look. He's reading the newspaper.''

''He's pretending to read the paper, but he's much more intrigued by you.''

Karen pushed up the sleeves on her white blouse and checked her watch, more out of nervousness than real interest in the time, although she did have an impending appointment. A very important appointment. ''Doesn't he have a job?''

''Oh, yes. He's very successful, or so Daniel tells me. Some sort of independent financial consultant. He travels all over the world.''

Daniel, another cousin, was the son of Karen's father's twin brother, Paul, and the reason why the sheikh had attended the welcome party. ''That sounds fairly suspect to me.''

Maria propped her elbows on the counter and rested her cheeks on her palms. ''Job or no job, he's wealthy. And royalty.'' She suddenly came to attention. ''And he's heading this way.''

Karen froze, as if adhered to the counter at her back by the icy apprehension traveling up and down her spine.

''May we help you, Sheikh Saalem?''

Staring straight ahead, Karen heard the creak of the

counter stool yet still couldn't force herself to turn around.

''It would help me greatly if you would call me Ash. In America, I prefer to dispose of the title, at least among friends. And I do consider the Barones to be my friends.''

''Of course,'' Maria said. ''Any friend of Daniel's is certainly a friend of ours. Right, Karen?''

Karen flinched at the sudden jab of Maria's elbow in her side. Realizing she had no room to run, she finally turned to face the sheikh. ''Yes. Friends. Of course.''

As far as grins went, Karen would qualify Ash Saalem's as awe-inspiring. Why did he have to be so annoyingly gorgeous?

''You're looking well today, Ms. Rawlins,'' he said in a voice as smooth and liquid as quicksilver.

He kept his eyes fixed on hers and Karen wanted to look away but decided to stand her ground. ''Thank you.''

''Are you enjoying your work here, Karen?''

Karen couldn't believe he had the audacity to call her by her first name. She couldn't believe her pulse had the nerve to quicken over hearing him say it. Of course, he'd been bold enough to kiss her that night, so why not dispense with all formality? ''As a matter of fact, I love working here. Very much.'' She forced an overly sweet smile, yet her lips felt stiff with the effort. ''Speaking of work, can I get you anything else?''

He leaned forward, bringing with him a trace of rich cologne and blatant self-assurance. ''What do you have in mind?''

Oh, no you don't. Karen was in no mood for playing the innuendo game. ''Maybe some gelato. It's very refreshing. Helps to cool one off.'' Ice cream was the only thing she planned to offer him today, or any day for that matter.

"What if I asked for some of your time? Perhaps dinner once you are through with your duties?"

"I really don't think—"

"Miss, I need some service over here."

Karen glanced at the end of the counter where a middle-aged businessman sporting a cheap suit and an edgy expression waited impatiently. She visually searched the area for Maria, who had conveniently disappeared.

"Excuse me," Karen said to the sheikh and headed to the customer. She took a pencil from the pocket of her apron along with the order pad. "What can I get for you, sir?"

The man's expression was pickle-sour. "A cup of coffee."

"Espresso, cappuccino or maybe—"

"Plain coffee, black, to go."

"Certainly. I've just started a fresh pot to brewing."

He released a gruff sigh. "I'm in a hurry."

So was Karen. In a hurry to get out of there before she did something inane like actually agree to Ash's offer of dinner. "It should only be a few more minutes."

"You have yet to answer my question, Karen."

Karen glanced at Ash then gave the grumpy guy her best smile. "Excuse me just a moment." She sidestepped until she was again in front of the sheikh, feeling as if she were caught in a verbal volley. "I don't have time for dinner. I have somewhere I have to be after work."

"Somewhere important?"

More than he realized. "You could say that."

"Then this is somewhere that I would not be welcome?"

Karen decided he would probably be more than welcome at the fertility clinic, at least to provide a donation. Who in their right mind would turn him down? Of course, she would. Not that she intended to reveal what she was about to do. "It's an appointment. A doctor's appointment."

Concern called out from his dark eyes. "Are you ill?"

"Just a routine exam." Not exactly a lie. "I'm fine."

His frown dissolved into a stop-and-drop grin. "I would attest to that without the benefit of an examination, although I would not mind further investigation."

"Is that coffee ready yet?" the sour man barked.

Karen welcomed the interruption on one level. On the other hand, she felt trapped between two persistent men intent on shredding her last nerve. She afforded the stranger a polite smile. "One more minute and the coffee should be done."

He slapped his palm on the counter. "I don't have another minute, so if you'll quit talking to your boyfriend and get me my coffee, then I can get out of here. Some of us have jobs to do."

Karen clenched her teeth and spoke through them. "I understand, sir, but the coffee's not quite done yet. Could I get you a glass of water while you're waiting?" Would you like to wear it? she wanted to say and would have except she'd been told the customer was always right. Even the fussy ones.

"I don't want any damned water. I want my coffee."

Ash had seemed unaffected by the jerk until that moment when a dangerous look came across his face. He took off his jacket, systematically laid it across the stool next to him and pushed up the sleeves of his shirt. Karen froze from fear that the sheikh was about to engage in fisticuffs with the irritable stranger. Instead, he walked around the counter, picked up a paper to-go cup, filled it with the last of the remaining lukewarm coffee from the previous pot, then turned and slid it in front of the man.

"This is in exchange for your absence," he said in a low, menacing voice. "I realize there is no sign on the door indicating this establishment does not serve jackasses, but rest assured, that will be remedied after your departure."

The man scowled. "You arrogant son of a—"

"My arrogance should not concern you. If you fail to leave the premises in thirty seconds, however, you should concern yourself with what I might do to encourage your departure."

The man stormed out the door sans coffee, sending Karen and Ash an acid look through the window.

When Karen could finally speak, she turned and stood toe-to-toe with the prince. She would estimate him to be not more than six feet tall, but in the small space that separated them, he seemed as massive as the ancient oak in the backyard of her former Montana home. "Was that really necessary?"

"I refuse to tolerate insolence, particularly when a woman is the target of disrespect."

Oh, good grief. "I really didn't need to be rescued."

His expression remained solemn. "My apologies. I tend to forget chivalry has lost its appeal in America."

Karen felt somewhat remorseful since she realized he'd had honorable intentions. She also felt somewhat tense when he continued to survey her with his extreme dark eyes. The least she could do was thank him. "I appreciate your good intentions."

His features softened into a look that could only be described as patently provocative. "You could show your gratitude by having dinner with me tonight."

"I told you I don't have the time." She didn't have the guts.

Maria suddenly appeared and eyed them both standing behind the counter, face-to-face. "Karen, did you hire the sheikh while I was downstairs?"

Karen reached under the counter and snatched up her car keys. "He was helping out with a rowdy customer."

"How nice of you, Ash," Maria said. "Wasn't it nice of him, Karen?"

Karen's stubborn gaze came to rest on Ashraf Saalem once more. Certain aspects of him were very nice. Nice and sexy. But she wouldn't describe his eyes as nice. More like lethal in a most sensual sense.

She unhooked her gaze from the sheikh and addressed Maria. "Is Mimi here yet? I really need to go swoon." Stupid, stupid mouth. "I mean I need to go soon. To my appointment."

Maria grinned and flipped her hand toward the front door. "Go ahead. I can handle it until she gets here. We still have some slack time before the evening crush."

Karen felt the pull of an inadvisable crush on an overbearing, arrogant, exotic prince. Stupid, stupid libido.

Keys in hand, she headed toward the door before Ash had another chance to knock her resistance out from under her.

"I will be in touch, Karen."

Karen gripped the door handle, intending to exit, but halted at the sound of his enticing voice. She only hesitated for a moment before rushing to her car and speeding off before she was tempted to go back and accept his offer. Before she gave in to those magnetic eyes and that seriously sinful voice. Before she forgot that she had no desire to become involved with any man, especially a man who considered himself her protector.

Thank heavens she had managed a quick getaway.

* * *

Ashraf Saalem had no intention of letting Karen Rawlins get away. From the moment he'd laid eyes on her at the welcome soiree, from the instant he had spontaneously kissed her, he had wanted her. He still wanted her and he intended to have her, even if forced to practice the utmost in patience.

Ash was not known for his patience. He would never have gained his own fortune had it not been for persistence. He would have never left the security of his family's business and come to America had he been willing to endure his father's demands.

"Oh, darn."

Maria Barone's mild oath brought Ash's attention to her. "A problem?"

She held up a black leather handbag. "Karen was in such a rush that she left her purse."

Ash saw Karen's carelessness as an opportunity to utilize a bit more strategy to convince her to see him again, this time alone. "I will be most happy to return it to her."

"Now?"

"Yes. I would think she might need it since I assume it contains her driver's license and any means she would have to pay for services."

Maria looked hesitant, wary. "You have a point. But I'm not sure she'll be too thrilled if I tell you where she's going."

"She mentioned a doctor's appointment."

"She did?"

Maria need not know that the revelation had come after some coercion on his part. "Do you know the whereabouts of the doctor's office?"

A slight-of-frame, gray-haired woman breezed up to

Maria and offered, "She asked me directions to Industrial Drive at Blakenship yesterday, the two hundred block, so I'm guessing that's the location."

Maria gave the waitress a scolding look. "Mimi, Karen might not like you passing on that information."

The woman rolled her eyes. "She has to have her purse, doesn't she? Besides, I don't think he's going to pilfer her credit cards."

"I guess you're right," Maria said.

Ash held out his hand to Maria and she finally relinquished the bag to him. "You may trust that I will find Ms. Rawlins and deliver it safely."

"Good luck," Maria said.

Ash wasn't one to rely on luck, but he would use his powers of persuasion. He gave the two women a polite nod. "I'm certain I will be back soon."

The lady named Mimi favored him with a smile. "I'm sure you will since Karen works here. That missy is a looker, all right."

Without responding, Ash left the building, unable to hold back his own smile over his good fortune. He had something Karen Rawlins needed, and she had something he wanted. Quite simply he wanted her. At least this was a beginning.

On that thought, Ash strode to the silver Rolls-Royce Corniche parked at the curb, slipped into the seat and drove away, his impatience escalating as he wove through heavy downtown traffic. After what seemed an interminable amount of time, he turned off onto the side street Maria had mentioned and approached a redbrick building that appeared to be a clinic.

Ash pulled into the parking lot and when he noticed the sign that read Milam Fertility Center, he assumed he'd come to the wrong place. Then, near the entrance, he caught sight of a blue compact car that resembled the one he'd seen Karen drive away in at Baronessa's.

He took the first available space several rows away, grabbed her purse and left the car to take his place by the hood where he could still view her vehicle. Presuming she had already entered, he decided to wait until she came out even if it took several hours. He had many questions to ask Karen, the most important being why she had chosen a clinic that catered to those intending a pregnancy. Then the sedan's door opened and Karen stepped from the car.

Ash saw his chance and strode across the parking lot, finding her bent halfway in, halfway out of the car. He paused a moment to study the bow of her hips and the pleasing shape of her legs extending from the skirt she wore as she conducted a search for, most likely, the handbag.

"Are you looking for this?"

She barely avoided bumping her head as she spun around to face him. "What are you doing here?" Her voice held a note of shock, as did her expression.

He dangled the purse before her. "I have come to return this to you."

She snatched it from his hand. "Thank you. I didn't realize I'd left it."

Obviously. "Now it is your turn to answer a question." He sent a direct look at the nearby sign. "What are you doing here?"

She worked the bag's strap round and round her slender fingers. "I told you I have—"

"An appointment, I know. But what business would you have at this establishment? Are you applying for employment?"

She looked almost alarmed. "Of course not." After

closing the door with a thrust of her bottom, she leaned back against it, looking quite annoyed. "You shouldn't concern yourself with why I'm here."

Her guardedness frustrated Ash though he had no call to interrogate her. But he had to know why she was here. "I would greatly like to understand your purpose for being at this particular place."

"You don't need to understand. This is my business, not yours."

"It is my business if you are involved with someone with whom you plan to have a child, if that is your reason for being here."

"Why is that your business?"

"Because I would cease to insist that you see me socially. I would not want to intrude on another man's territory."

Her gold-green eyes turned to feminine fire. "For your information, Sheikh Saalem, I am no man's territory. In this day and time, a woman doesn't need a man to have a baby, at least not all of a man." By the discomfort in Karen's expression, Ash discerned that she regretted the revelation.

He streaked a hand over his jaw, not quite certain what to make of Karen's disclosure. "Then you plan to have a child on your own?"

She tipped up her chin in defiance. "Yes, I do. Artificial insemination."

That did not set well with Ash. He understood the need for the procedure in some instances, but not in this case. "Do you mean insemination with some stranger's sperm?"

A blush spread across her cheeks. "I don't care to discuss sperm with a sheikh."

"But you would consider having a child by a man you know nothing about?"

"Yes, and that's my prerogative. I'm thirty-one and I'm not getting any younger. It's the right time in my life to do this."

Ash pondered her words, her purpose. Yes, he definitely had something Karen needed. Services he no doubt would be willing to give her, with great pleasure. And she had something else he wanted as well. The ability to have a child, the means for him to settle into a permanent relationship with a woman whom he found both intelligent and alluring. He had waited many years to find that particular someone since his father had thwarted his first attempt.

"Perhaps I could assist you in the matter," he said.

Her eyes went wide. "You mean you're willing to make a donation for me to use?"

"I have no desire to share my affections with a plastic receptacle. I prefer making a child the way nature intended for a man and woman to procreate."

Karen shook her head. "No way. I'm not going to allow…well, allow…*that.*"

Ash moved closer and brushed a lock of wavy brown hair from her shoulder. He suspected Karen enjoyed a challenge, much like him, and if he had to use that device, then so be it. "Are you afraid?"

The willful look she gave him verified his assumption. "Of course I'm not afraid. Why would I be?"

He braced a hand on the car and leaned forward. "Perhaps you fear what you might feel if you allowed me to make love to you. What we might experience together."

He heard a slight catch in her breath, the only sign she had been affected by his words. "It wouldn't be a good idea, that's all."

"It is an exceptional idea. For some time now I've considered having a family of my own. This would benefit us both."

Her sigh brimmed with impatience. "I only want a baby, not a relationship."

"A baby who would not know his father? I believe that if you search your soul, you would not want this for your child, considering what you have recently learned about your father's kidnapping."

Karen studied the toe of her functional black canvas shoes, avoiding his gaze. "I don't have a choice. I want a baby more than anything."

With a fingertip, Ash nudged her chin up until she looked at him. He saw only indecision in her eyes, not total refusal. Enough to propel him forward in his planning. "I am offering you a choice. I am willing to father your child."

She eyed him with suspicion. "And exactly what would you expect in return?"

He had given his heart to a woman once, and only once. He had no more left to give in that respect. But he could give Karen the baby she desired and a comfortable home, a secure future. "I want to have you as my wife."

She frowned. "That's nuts. We don't know each other."

"What better way to become acquainted?"

"I don't want to get married. I almost made that mistake not long ago." Again she looked chagrined, as if she had revealed too much.

Ash had no call to be envious of another man who'd had Karen's affections in the past, yet surprisingly he was. No matter. If given the chance, he would attempt to make her forget any former liaison, especially one that appeared to have caused her pain. He could personally relate to that concept.

In order to do that, he must convince her that marriage would be favorable for them both, even if it meant proposing terms that were anything but amenable. ''Perhaps we should have an agreement. If you decide not to continue the marriage, you are under no obligation to uphold the arrangement. You would be free to leave after the birth of our child.''

''You mean divorce?''

The word sounded harsh in Ash's ears. It went against everything he believed. ''Yes.''

She worked her bottom lip between her teeth several times before saying, ''I take it you would want to stay involved with the baby after the agreement ends.''

He would do everything in his power to make certain that there would be no need to discuss custody of their child. He would do everything humanly possible to prevent their marriage from ending. ''Of course. Would you not want that?''

''I suppose that would be best.''

Ash sensed impending victory. ''Then we are agreed?''

''No.'' She straightened and slipped the purse's strap over one thin shoulder. ''I need to keep my appointment. Weigh all my options until I've reached a decision.''

Ash pushed away from the sedan and gestured toward the building's entrance, not quite ready to concede defeat. ''Go inside with my blessing, Karen. And while you are there, think of me.'' He slipped his arms around her waist. ''Think of us. Consider what I am offering you, a father your child will know. The means to create life through an act that will give us both pleasure.''

He pulled her closer and kissed her—a kiss meant to

persuade, to tantalize, to keep him foremost in her mind. Her lips were firm against his, but with only slight coaxing, Karen finally opened to him and he took supreme advantage, slipping his tongue inside the soft, sweet heat of her mouth, but only once. A brief glimpse of how it could be between them.

With great effort, Ash stepped away from her, withdrew a business card from his pocket and pressed into her palm with an added stroke of his thumb over her wrist. "Here are the numbers where I can be reached when you make your decision. Decide wisely."

Karen remained as still as a pillar as Ash walked away. Hopefully good judgment would reign and she would see the logic in his offer and agree to his proposal. If not right away, then he would simply have to try harder to persuade her.

Two

The man knew no shame.

Karen couldn't believe that Ash Saalem had kissed her in a wide-open parking lot that afternoon. She couldn't believe that he'd offered to father her child. She couldn't believe that she was actually considering his proposition.

After pouring a glass of Chianti, Karen strolled into the living room and slumped onto the sofa in hopes of clearing her mind. She loved the fourth-floor brownstone apartment generously provided by the Barones. Gina had decorated the place beautifully with Italian silk sofas, an antique writing table, Turkish rugs. But the elegant furnishings and accoutrements wouldn't fair well with an active toddler.

She was getting way ahead of herself. First she had to conceive, *then* she could decide on the living arrangements. At present the conception should be her top priority. That and Ash's offer, not his masterful mouth. She needed to get the kiss off her mind so she could think clearly, not a measly mission by any means. Neither was deciding the best option for having a baby.

She sipped the wine and thought about the day's events. During her appointment at the clinic, she had been instructed on what the procedure entailed and the possible cost, emotionally and physically, if she wasn't successfully inseminated after several attempts. She had sorted through some sample profiles of prospective donors, most too good to be true. She had watched several couples in the waiting room looking anxious and hopeful—and in love.

Maybe Ash was right. Did she really want to bring a baby into the world not knowing its heritage, considering she'd grown up not knowing the truth about hers? Could she really trust that the sperm donors were being completely honest? After all, she had recently learned that much of what she'd believed about her family lineage had been skewed by dishonesty.

Feeling emotionally drained, Karen set her wineglass on a coaster on the end table and stretched out on the sofa on her back. She'd eaten a light supper of pasta and vegetables but hadn't tasted much of anything. Too much to think about, too little time. If she decided to go through with the insemination, she needed to make the arrangements in less than three days since that would be right before the most fertile time during her cycle. The same held true if she decided to accept the sheikh's arrangement.

Just thinking about making love with Ash brought about a round of chills mixed with a flash-fire heat. She couldn't deny that the idea held some appeal. She also couldn't deny that his kiss had left its mark on her libido. Both kisses.

The doorbell buzzed, sending Karen off the sofa in a rush. She experienced a prickly surge of panic thinking Ash might have decided to pay her a visit expecting an answer she wasn't quite ready to give. It would be just like him to show up, unannounced, and come upon her wearing a threadbare gray sweatshirt and equally ragged black leggings. She would send him on his way—as long as he kept his mouth to himself.

As she looked through the peephole and saw Maria at her threshold, Karen was relieved and maybe just a teeny bit disappointed that Ash hadn't come by to convince her with more kisses. Absolutely ridiculous.

Karen opened the door to her cousin and smiled. "Hey, you. What brings you to the top floor this time of night?"

"Just wanted to visit," Maria said, her shoulders slumped as if she carried the obligations of the universe.

Karen was immediately concerned, considering Maria had looked incredibly tired of late. The gelateria required long hours and hard work, especially for Maria, its manager. A lot of responsibility for a young woman, yet Maria, even at the tender age of twenty-three, handled it remarkably well. Or so Karen had believed until tonight.

"Come on in," Karen said and gestured toward the sofa. "Take a load off. I was having a glass of wine. Join me."

Maria dropped onto the sofa and tipped her head back. "No wine for me."

"Maybe something else, then? I could fix us some tea."

"No thanks."

"Are you okay? You look exhausted." And she sounded depressed.

She shrugged. "I took the stairs from my apartment

instead of the elevator. I'm a little winded, but otherwise I'm fine.''

Maria always climbed the two flights to visit Karen on the fourth floor and she'd never even broken a minor sweat. Something was seriously wrong, and Karen aimed to get to the bottom of Maria's distress.

Karen sat on the wing chair facing the sofa. ''Okay, so what's up?''

Maria managed a faint smile. ''You go first. I want to hear about your baby-making appointment.''

''Not that much to tell, really. I had an interview, discussed financial terms, then I got a sneak preview of perspective sperm donors.''

''That must have been interesting.''

Not as interesting as Ash's suggestion. Karen wasn't sure she needed to burden Maria with her dilemma, but she had no one else to turn to. Maria had become a good friend to Karen, a confidante, and she always seemed so wise.

''I have another offer on the table,'' Karen began. ''In terms of a father for my child.''

Maria instantly perked up. ''Really? That wouldn't happen to have come from a handsome Arabian prince, would it?''

She eyed Maria suspiciously. ''Did he tell you?''

''I promise he didn't tell me anything. I only knew that he was bent on returning your purse to you.''

''So that's how he knew where to find me.''

''I'm sorry, Karen.'' Maria looked more than a tad contrite. ''Actually, Mimi gave him the directions and I gave him the purse. He's very persuasive.''

''No kidding,'' Karen muttered.

''He's also absolutely head over heels for you.''

''Good heavens, Maria. I barely know the man.'' But

if the sheikh had his way, that would be remedied shortly on a very intimate level.

"Exactly what did his offer entail?" Maria asked.

"He's willing to father my child. The natural way."

Laying a hand on her chest, Maria said, "Oh, my. That could be great fun."

Exactly Karen's current thought, and her quandary. "Fun, yes. Wise, I doubt it."

"And he was serious?"

"Very serious. But he won't do it unless we're married. He did say that we could make it a conditional marriage and if I decide to end it, I can after the baby's born."

"Are you going to do it?"

Was she? The terms of the arrangement didn't seem as absurd once she'd voiced them to Maria. "I don't know. Part of me thinks that I would be a total fool to do it. Another part of me…well, that part—"

"Thinks you'd be a fool not to know the father considering the blank spaces in your own family. Not to mention, the sheikh probably has incredible genes and making a baby with him would be an out-of-this-world experience."

Karen couldn't hold back her smile. "Yes, that's basically what that part of me is saying. The feminine part." She turned serious again. "But he's got that whole macho thing going. That was very apparent when he took it upon himself to come to my rescue today at the shop. I could have handled that guy myself."

"He was only concerned for your welfare."

"I understand that, to a point. But he's too in control and I couldn't tolerate living with someone who tries to keep a tight rein on me all the time."

Maria shifted on the couch, looking unquestionably

uncomfortable. "That could be a problem only if you're not clear on what you expect from him. Who knows? It might even lead to a permanent relationship."

"Not likely. We're from two entirely different worlds."

Maria murmured, "Stranger things have happened." She pushed her dark, shoulder-length hair back with one hand. "Regardless, every child should know both its mother and father if at all possible. Family is everything."

Karen understood that all too well having recently lost the only family she'd ever known. And she also surmised that something was terribly wrong with Maria considering the hint of sadness in her voice. Feeling totally selfish, she said, "Your turn now, cousin dear. Tell me what's bothering you."

A steady stream of tears rolled down Maria's face, catching Karen off guard, inciting her concern. "Maria, what's wrong?"

"It's a long, painful story, Karen."

Karen moved from the chair and seated herself beside Maria on the sofa. "I have all night. Please tell me what's going on. I'm really worried about you."

Maria lifted her plain white blouse and rested a hand on her abdomen. "This is what's going on."

Karen noticed a prominent belly bulge beneath the waistband of Maria's black slacks. Realization suddenly dawned and it had nothing to do with her cousin putting on a few extra pounds from sneaking too much gelato. "Are you—"

"Pregnant? Yes. And no one knows. No one can know. At least no one except you."

More confused than ever, Karen let a few moments of

silence pass between them while she allowed the shock to subside. "Who is he?"

Maria sighed. "Someone I've been secretly seeing since January."

"Secretly? Is he married, Maria?"

"Worse. He's a Conti."

Shock came calling again as Karen tried to assimilate the information. Her cousin had just told her that she was pregnant by a man who belonged to a family that had been sworn enemies of the Barones for decades. Both families—the Contis and the Barones—seemed determined to hang on to old recriminations. No wonder Maria didn't want anyone to know.

"His name is Steven," Maria continued. "He's beautiful and caring and I'm totally in love with him."

"He sounds wonderful, Maria. Other than the family thing, what's the problem?"

"The family thing is the problem. With so much going on of late—the gelato sabotage that happened right before you came, the warehouse fire—everything's in an uproar because some of the family think the Contis are behind it. They would never accept our relationship. It would only tear us and the families farther apart if they found out about us."

"Maybe your relationship and this baby will help settle the rift."

"I can't imagine that happening, at least not now. In fact, I'm not even up to dealing with it. I want to get away for a while, somewhere out of town. Think things through. And that's what I intend to do, right away, since I'm already starting to show."

"How far along are you?" Karen asked.

"Four months."

Another surprise to Karen. But come to think of it,

Maria had started wearing her blouse over her slacks, something Karen hadn't given much thought until now. "If I can do something, just name it."

"I'll need you to handle the shop in my absence."

"Of course." Karen would do anything for Maria considering what Maria had done for her—made her feel welcome and wanted, as if she were a sister, not a long-lost cousin. "Does Steven know about your plans to leave?"

"He doesn't even know about the baby."

Stunned, Karen asked, "Why not?"

"It wouldn't be fair to lay this on him now. Not until I decide what I'm going to do."

"You're not considering giving up the baby, are you?"

Maria looked mortified. "No! I love this baby and even if it doesn't work out between Steven and me, I'll at least have a part of him with me always."

"Do you really have so little hope that you and Steven can make this work?"

"I want to hope, Karen. Really, I do, but I'm afraid the relationship is doomed. We have too many obstacles to overcome."

Karen's heart went out to Maria. Hopefully a little time away would clear her mind. "Where do you plan to go?"

"That's why I'm here. Do you still own your old house in Montana?"

"I've recently sold it to a friend of the family."

"Then I guess that's out."

Karen thought a moment and considered another option. The perfect place for a sabbatical. "I have two dear friends in Silver Valley, the Calderones. They have a wonderful ranch and I'm sure they would love to have you as a guest for as long as you'd like."

Maria's expression brightened. "Do you really think so?"

"I'm almost positive but I'll give them a call in the morning and run it past them."

Maria grasped Karen's hand. "You're a lifesaver, Karen. I'm so happy to have you in the family."

"I'm happy to be in the family." And Karen was. Only a few months before she had felt totally alone. Now she had her understanding cousin to lean on as well as other new friends. She also had…Ash? The sneaky sheikh once again had wriggled his way into her psyche.

Coming to her feet, Maria stretched with her hands on the small of her back. "Lately every muscle in my body protests if I stand or sit too long."

Karen rose. "You need to try and get some rest."

"I haven't been able to sleep well."

Karen doubted she would sleep all that well tonight either with so much weighing on her mind. "Take a hot bath and relax. Works for me. I'll let you know what the Calderones say, but you can probably consider it a done deal."

Maria gave Karen a quick, heartfelt hug. "Thanks for making the arrangements. I owe you one."

"Just come back soon. I'm going to miss you."

"I'll miss you, too. But you have to promise me that no matter what, you can't tell Steven anything. Or the family. I don't want anyone to know why I've left."

"Won't everyone be worried about you?"

"I'll leave the family a note explaining I need some time away. Steven, too. And now that that's settled, what are you going to do about Ash's offer?"

"I have no idea. I have a lot to consider."

Maria walked to the door then faced Karen. "No matter what you decide, you know I'll support you. But I do hope you give the proposal some serious consideration. It would be so wonderful for your baby to have a relationship with its father.''

Karen's heart ached for Maria who hadn't been able to openly share her joy with the father of her child or her family. Recalling the missing links to her own family chain, Karen could no longer deny the importance of having both parents actively involved. She also couldn't deny that Sheikh Ashraf Saalem would probably be a prime candidate for producing top-notch offspring. And she definitely couldn't deny that he would be the prime candidate for providing the utmost in pleasure, either. Annoyingly, that thought excited her.

Too much to think about, too little time.

''I've always known you to be a man of few words, Ash, but today you're quieter than usual.''

Ash looked up from his half-eaten room service fare to find Daniel Barone scrutinizing him with unconcealed curiosity. ''I have much on my mind at present.'' So much that food had lost all appeal.

''This mood of yours doesn't have anything to do with my investments, does it?''

His current state had nothing to do with monetary measures and everything to do with one particular woman. ''I asked you here today solely for the sake of camaraderie, not business.''

''Good. I was beginning to assume you were about to tell me I'm destined for poverty, the reason why we're eating in privacy instead of a restaurant.''

Ash had asked Daniel to join him for lunch in his penthouse suite to make certain he was accessible should Karen call. To this point, it had yet to happen. The later the hour, the more concerned Ash had become that perhaps Karen had decided to utilize the fertility clinic. For all he knew, she could be there now, becoming impregnated by some stranger.

"As always, your investments are thriving," Ash assured his friend. "You will continue to be a very wealthy man."

Pushing back from the dining table, Daniel tossed his napkin aside, looking pleased. "That's great to know even though I have everything a man could need with my new wife."

Ash felt a little twinge of envy over his friend's good fortune in finding a suitable mate. "Then I can presume your honeymoon went well?"

Daniel presented a roguish grin. "Oh, yeah. Very well. But it's far from over. Just ask Phoebe. For such a quiet lady, she's certainly full of surprises."

Ash predicted that the not-so-quiet Karen could be full of pleasant surprises as well. If only he would be afforded the opportunity to find out. "I'm happy that you are pleased with your choice."

"And to think I tried to fix you and Phoebe up at Karen's party," Daniel said. "Good thing you didn't hit it off."

A very good thing, Ash decided, not that Phoebe wasn't an attractive woman. But that night Karen had garnered his complete attention. Admittedly, he had wanted her in a very elemental way. He still wanted her. Yet with each passing moment he saw his opportunity to have her dwindling.

"I am still surprised that you've married, considering your former habits," Ash said.

Daniel frowned. "If you're referring to previous women, you're a fine one to talk. You've had more than your share."

"True, but I have met someone who could possibly put that to an end."

"Someone special?"

"Your cousin Karen."

Daniel slapped his palm on the table, effectively rattling the silverware. "You know, Phoebe swore this was going to happen but I never thought it would go beyond the night you met. Karen didn't seem too happy when you kissed her in the reception line."

"It was a simple show of welcome."

"It was a simple come-on, if you ask me. So how long have you and Karen been an item?"

"I'm not certain I understand your meaning."

"How long have you been seeing each other?"

Ash was unsure how to respond. "We've been negotiating."

"Negotiating? That's a weird term for dating."

"Actually, we have gone beyond the dating phase."

Daniel released a wry chuckle. "I have to hand it to you, Ash. You work fast."

"I've asked her to be my wife."

"Make that from zero to sixty in a matter of seconds. When did this all come about?"

"I've intended to marry for some time now. Karen is the perfect prospect."

"Yeah, Karen's a nice woman. Not too shabby in the looks department, either."

"I beg your pardon?"

"She's very attractive."

"I would have to agree with you in that respect."

"So when's the wedding?"

As far as Ash was concerned, today would not be soon enough. "Unfortunately she has yet to give me her answer. I'm not certain that she sees the mutual benefits that marriage will bring.''

Daniel scowled. ''Well, hell, Ash, if that's the way you proposed, it's not surprising she hasn't bothered to answer you.''

''It's a bit more complex than a simple proposal. Karen and I have both expressed our desire to have a child. We've discussed having one together. I have insisted that we marry for the sake of that child.''

''Then this doesn't have anything to do with love?''

Ash didn't expect Daniel to fully understand. Why would he when he was so obviously in love with his wife? ''I am very fond of Karen, and I have every intention of making a comfortable life for her and our child in a secure, permanent relationship.''

''You make it sound like a retirement fund.'' Daniel shook his head. ''I'm not sure how well this is going to work, putting the cart before the horse.''

When Ash showed his confusion with a frown, Daniel added, ''Having the marriage and a baby before you have a commitment that involves two people who care about each other.''

''I'm a realist, Daniel. At times it is necessary to accept that the choices we make should be based on what is best for all concerned, not on emotions.''

''So you're saying that all you expect is a continuing fondness for Karen?''

''I expect nothing beyond what I know to be true, that we will marry in order to produce a child. I can't deny that I find Karen to be a very desirable, passionate woman. I plan to enjoy those aspects.''

Daniel's expression reflected concern. ''When the passion fades, I hope that something more exists. Otherwise, you might be in for a tough life together.''

Ash gave Daniel's words some consideration, and though he found wisdom in them, he couldn't allow himself to become entangled in emotions, especially if Karen decided that she wanted to dissolve the marriage after the birth of their child despite his efforts to dissuade her. Before he could concern himself with that, she must first agree to be his wife.

"And one more thing, Ash," Daniel said. "The Barones take family very seriously. Karen has only been a member for a short time but she's been completely accepted."

"I understand." And he did. Ash realized all too well the strength of family ties, or in his case, chains.

Daniel's expression went stern. "And just so you know, you might be a good friend, but if you do anything to hurt her, you will have to answer not only to the rest of the family but to me as well."

He had no intention of hurting Karen. He had no intention of allowing her to cause him pain, either. "You can rest assured that I will take very good care of her."

"Speaking of family," Daniel said, "what is yours going to think about you marrying an American?"

Ash saw no reason to tell them immediately. Perhaps later, after the birth of their child. Or perhaps he would call his father following the marriage ceremony if only to inform him that he had not been able to interfere this time.

Ash had waited thirty-six years for the moment when he could prove that the king of Zhamyr no longer had control over his son's life. "I no longer concern myself with my family's approval. And I have no obligations as heir since that duty falls on my eldest brother."

The phone rang and Daniel immediately rose in response. "I'll get it. I told Phoebe to call when she's ready for me to come home."

Ash couldn't hold back a cynical smile brought about by more envy. "I see she has you shackled."

Daniel turned with his hand on the phone. "We haven't tried shackles yet, but you never know." He answered with a brief hello, said, "Send her up," then dropped the receiver onto its cradle.

"I take it your wife has decided to personally escort you home," Ash said.

"It's not my wife who's on her way up here."

"Then who?"

"The woman you intend to make your wife."

Three

With every solitary ping of the elevator climbing to the top floor of the New Regents Hotel, Karen's heart beat double-time in her chest.

She was the lone occupant in the car with the exception of a starched and polished attendant who stood in the corner wearing a blue-tailored suit and a poker-faced expression. More than likely, he thought her to be one of the catering staff since she was dressed for work in a black skirt and tailored white blouse. Of course, she was about to meet with a prince who could very well expect her to cater to his every whim. But not if she could help it. She only had one goal in mind—a father for her child. And to conduct her own little interview to make sure that the sheikh fit the father bill.

Karen felt totally out of her element when the doors opened with quiet efficiency to a hallway covered in rich red carpet. She doubted it had been rolled out for her, simple Karen Rawlins from Nowhere, Montana.

The attendant stepped out and kept his hand on the door to prevent its closure. With his free hand, he indicated the entrance at the end of the corridor. "Sheikh Saalem's penthouse, madam."

She hoped he'd meant madam in a polite sense and didn't mistakenly believe she was there to service the sheikh. Surely not. Now if he knew she was wearing skimpy zebra-striped underwear—her one secret indulgence—she could understand where he might make that assumption. But unless he had X-ray vision, he had no way of knowing that.

The man cleared his throat and made a flicking motion on his chin. Did he expect a tip? Karen considered supplying a verbal one—lose the toupee.

Just when Karen reached into her bag for a few bucks, he said, "Mustard, miss."

Only then did Karen realize she was sporting the remnants of a sandwich she had consumed in record time during her drive to the hotel. Embarrassed, she used the oval mirror across the hall to remove the yellow chin smudge with a napkin she'd stuffed in her purse. While she was at it, she secured the clip holding her hair in a loose upsweep then checked her lipstick. Luckily it was still there, and so was the attendant. From the mirror's reflection, she noticed that he was ogling her. Ogling her legs, to be more accurate.

She rolled her eyes to the ornate ceiling, turned and forced a smile. "Thank you. That will be all."

He gave her a brusque nod, backed into the elevator and closed the doors. How nice that he'd immediately left with little effort on her part, Karen thought. Dismissed with nothing more than a simple command.

Standing before the double doors to the sheikh's suite, clutching her basic black bag to her chest, Karen acknowledged she could get used to saying "That will be all" like some demanding debutante, especially if it encouraged others to do her bidding.

She seriously doubted it would work on Ash Saalem. She also doubted she would be able to get any words out once she faced his high-voltage sensuality, live and in person. But last night, after weighing Maria's advice, she'd decided to go through with the arrangement—if Ash satisfactorily answered her questions.

Yes, I will marry you and have your baby. That will be all.

Slipping the strap of her purse over her shoulder, Karen pressed the buzzer and sucked in a deep breath, expecting to be met by Ash. She certainly didn't expect to be greeted by her cousin Daniel.

"What are you doing here?" she asked in a remarkably calm tone despite her surprise.

Daniel stepped into the hall and gave her a wily grin. "Visiting with a friend. What are you doing here? Business or pleasure?"

Karen had no idea what Daniel had learned from Ash and frankly, she wasn't sure she wanted to know. From the moment she'd met him, Daniel had stepped into the role of the big brother Karen had never had. A big brother who delighted in teasing her. She refused to provide fodder for the ridicule mill. "I'm here on business." Not exactly a fib.

Daniel rubbed his jaw and his grin deepened. "Is Ash going to check out your portfolio?"

"Something like that." As much as she cherished Daniel, she wanted him to leave. She was anxious enough without his prodding. "Tell Phoebe I said hi, will you?"

"Sure." Daniel leaned forward, lowered his voice and said, "Don't forget the Do Not Disturb sign."

That will be all. "It's business, Daniel."

"If you say so." Daniel departed, taking his skeptical grin with him, leaving Karen alone with the sheikh who now stood at the door looking calm and composed, and subtly sinful in his casual tan polo shirt and black slacks.

"Come in," he said with a sweeping gesture.

Karen passed by Ash while maintaining enough distance between them to prevent inadvertently touching him. The pleasant scent emanating from him teased her senses, a one-of-a-kind fragrance that smelled a lot like incense, exotic but not overbearing. It reminded her of the patchouli oil Sunrise Bowers, Silver Valley's lone hippie and video store manager, had bathed in. It had that certain kind of distinctiveness, and Karen imagined it bore some equally unique name. Arabian Nights, Desert Sunset, Sex in the Sand.

Good grief.

To avoid looking at Ash, Karen turned her attention to the suite's opulent living area. A row of French doors opening onto a verandah revealed the downtown Boston skyline and the still overcast skies.

To her right, she noted a cherry wood dining table littered with lunch remains, to her left a sitting area with tan leather-covered sofas and chairs surrounding a small redbrick fireplace. And straight ahead, an open door revealed a king-size bed covered in a gold brocade spread. Quite different from the particle-board furniture, thin bath towels and faulty A/C she'd encountered in the motels where she had stayed on previous trips. Very nice decor indeed. Especially the bedroom and she definitely needed to stop looking at that.

The front door closed behind Karen, startling her. She

spun around and blurted, ''Nice place. Do you come here often?''

What was she thinking? She sounded like some barfly executing a bad pick-up line, not a smart, sophisticated woman bent on a mission. But Ash had a knack for making her totally tongue-tied and thought-challenged.

Ash took a couple of steps toward her. ''I reside here at the moment.''

''Where do you normally live?''

''Wherever my business happens to take me. I have no permanent residence.''

As if he were some sort of superpowered pulley, Karen moved toward him. She took her purse from her shoulder and hugged it again, as if it provided her some protection from his magnetism. ''Really? That seems odd, not having a place to call home.''

''I'm hoping to settle in Boston.''

He shortened the space between them with another stride, bringing them almost as close as they'd been the previous day behind Baronessa's counter. Karen had no real desire to move back though she probably should.

''Why are you here, Karen?''

''I want to ask you a few questions.''

Ash gestured toward the sofa. ''Would you like to be seated first?''

Sitting seemed like an extremely good idea. ''Sure.''

Karen claimed the end of the couch, expecting Ash to take the club chair across from her. Instead, he dropped onto the opposite end of the sofa and crossed one leg over the other, his arm draped on the back of the couch. He looked so at ease it almost angered Karen. So did her reaction to his nearness, the sudden images of him taking her down for the count on the nice plush woven rug at their feet.

At least her hormones wouldn't fail her when it came time to make a baby with him. She swallowed hard.

"You may speak first," Ash said.

Darn tootin', she would. She pointed at him. "That's it. That's exactly what I want to talk to you about."

"I'm not clear on your meaning."

"I think you should know upfront that for the past thirty-one years I've been inclined to express myself openly without anyone's permission."

He had the absolute gall to grin. "I find that to be one of your more intriguing qualities. But then I find everything about your mouth quite intriguing."

Karen's face went brush-fire hot. Back to the point. "My point is that I'm quite capable of taking care of myself and my needs in all respects."

"I have found that certain needs are better taken care of by others."

"Such as?" Boy, had she fallen right into that one.

His grin disappeared, replaced by a sultry, seductive expression. "Intimate needs."

Karen had no problem picturing Ash taking care of those needs. "I guess you could be right in that respect."

"Could be?"

"When it comes to conception. And that brings me to some important health issues. Do you have any known illness, disease, a family history of any diseases, mental illness?"

"I am in perfect health."

Karen would have to agree with that, or so it appeared. Very healthy indeedy. But those were only superficial aspects. "When was your last physical?"

"Two months ago with a prominent physician in New York. But if you are still concerned, I would be glad to allow you to examine my medical records, or anything else you might choose to examine."

"That won't be necessary." Loads of fun, but not necessary.

She searched her brain to try and remember exactly what the forms at the fertility clinic contained. Only one other question came to mind. "Do you have any hobbies?" Like that really mattered in the grand scheme of things.

"I like to ski, which is how I met your cousin Daniel. In the Pyrenees. I also enjoy the Alps."

"And your education?"

"I studied in France."

"Then you speak French?"

"Yes. I am quite proficient in several tongues."

She knew all about his proficient tongue, more than she'd ever bargained for. "Now, if we should happen to be successful in becoming pregnant—"

"We will be successful. My father has five sons and three daughters. Several of my brothers have that many offspring and so do my sisters. We, too, will have no trouble in that regard."

Karen only wanted one baby, not a brood. "I certainly hope you're right about your fertility. That it won't take more than one time for me to become pregnant."

"I admire your optimism, Karen, but I would think it best if we make more than one attempt."

She wasn't sure she'd survive more than one time, especially if he did justice to her overstimulated imagination. "Only if it's necessary. And after we achieve conception, I would prefer a platonic relationship." She figured he could very well rescind his offer after that little bomb.

"Then you do not wish me touch you after you become pregnant?"

"I think that's best."

Ash's stern expression said he believed otherwise. "I will agree not to touch you."

That was easy. Too easy. "Good."

"Unless you ask it of me."

Karen didn't plan on asking him any such thing. "I would really want to do it soon." Oh, cripes. "The wedding ceremony, I mean."

"Why the hurry?"

Karen felt a bout of stammering coming on so she drew in a deep breath and sat on her hands. When she became tense, she tended to flail them around. "The, uh, fertilization..." That sounded like a request for lawn service. "The attempt at conception needs to happen in the next four days at the latest. I'm sure we can use the courthouse." *Foot, get thee out of my mouth!* "I mean use the courthouse for the wedding, not the conception."

Ash looked as though he greatly enjoyed her floundering. "I agree that it might be inappropriate to make love on the courthouse lawn, although I admit it might be interesting to find a secluded place behind a hedge."

Vivid images filtered into Karen's brain like a clear cable channel that showed after-hours movies with titles that included words like "confessions" and "diaries." Visions of making love with Ash on the lawn, against the wall, in an exquisite king-size bed. Making a baby, she corrected. Love wasn't going to enter into it. Ever.

"If I do consent, will you make the arrangements or should I?" she asked.

His grin reappeared. "You wish me to find a hedge?"

He was obviously determined to keep her off balance, and quite possibly off her feet and in his bed after they were married. She refused to let that happen. "I'm referring to the *wedding* arrangements."

"I will handle all arrangements."

"Then I take it you wouldn't have a problem with having the wedding in the next four days?"

"I would gladly rearrange my schedule to accommodate you."

Not exactly what Karen had envisioned when she'd considered getting married, a quick service in a judge's chambers. But those were old, worn-out dreams that didn't matter any longer. Reality did. Practicality did. "I would want everything in writing."

His expression turned from seductive to solemn. "Do you not trust me?"

She didn't trust herself around him. "I think it's wise."

"I will have the papers drawn up."

"And that would include the clause about parting after the baby's born?"

Ash again looked more than a little miffed. "Yes, I would include that clause in the terms."

"Good." Karen quickly came to her feet. "I think that covers everything."

Ash rose to stand before her. "Then you have decided?"

"I have, and my answer is okay." There it was, and not so very painful after all.

Ash slipped his hands in his pockets as if he needed a means to control them. Unfortunately, Karen had no pockets in her skirt, not that she was going to touch him. Not that she wanted to touch him. Okay, maybe she did just a little.

"Are you saying we are agreed?" he asked with a hint of disbelief in his voice.

"Yes."

Ash's expression looked victorious. "I am pleased you see the advantages to our union."

She could think of one really nice advantage—the conception. "There is one more thing. When you make the arrangements, will you see if you can set it up around lunchtime?"

"That will be satisfactory. We could spend the rest of the afternoon meeting our objectives."

Coming from anyone else, that would have sounded like a dull, business proposition to Karen. Coming from Ash, it sounded like an invitation to sin. "I'm on the schedule to work evenings at the gelateria."

"You would not consider taking the day off?"

She thought about Maria and her impending departure. After making the call that morning to the Calderones who were thrilled to open their home to Maria, everything but the date and time had been set. Karen saw the wedding as the perfect opportunity for Maria to escape. Maria could serve as Karen's attendant then sneak away. A perfect plan.

But if Maria left that particular day, then Karen would have to work that evening, unless someone would be willing to pull a double shift. She had time to plan that later. Right now she needed to get back to her job before people started wondering where she was. Wouldn't they be shocked to know?

"Karen, is something troubling you?"

Karen brought her focus back to Ash who was studying her thoughtfully. "I'm just thinking about work. I'll see what I can do about taking the day off."

"Very good. I see no need to postpone the honeymoon."

Honeymoon? Well, she supposed that was what it was

in a sense. "I better get back to Baronessa now. I'm already late." She was already imagining their lovemaking in great detail, not a good idea at all.

Karen had almost made it to the door and merciful escape until Ash called her back. "Yes?"

"Perhaps we should seal our bargain with a kiss."

At least he'd asked her permission this time. "Do you really think that's necessary?" There went the flying hands. She clasped them tightly before her.

"I believe it would be favorable to familiarize ourselves with each other before we are in bed together. If my kisses continue to make you nervous then it will be much worse when I make love to you."

Karen's traitorous eyes targeted the bedroom at his back. "Your kisses don't make me nervous." Her shaky voice betrayed her.

"Then you should have no objections now."

When he moved closer, Karen's mouth started flapping along with her hands. "Let's keep it simple, shall we? I mean, this is more or less a business arrangement and—"

Ash caught both her hands and held them against his sturdy chest. "You are still nervous, Karen."

"I am not!" What a fish tale.

He took her hands, turned them over and kissed each palm. "You need not be anxious around me. I promise I will treat you with great care."

"I'm not breakable." At the moment she felt like delicate crystal, poised to shatter the moment he laid his mouth on hers.

He leaned forward, a thin thread away from her lips that began to twitch and tremble. "Nevertheless, I promise I will be very gentle with my hands." He leaned closer. "And with my mouth."

His deep, tempting voice threatened to make Karen

sway. She stiffened her frame, determined not to faint. "As long as you get the job done," she said with as much challenge as she could muster.

"I most certainly plan to get the job done, and quite sufficiently," he said, his voice barely above a whisper.

A long stretch of silence passed as Ash stared into Karen's eyes. She prepared for the fallout from his kiss, but the kiss didn't come. And then something incomprehensible happened to Karen. She kissed him first. Thoroughly, without the slightest hesitation.

She met his open mouth with an eagerness she didn't invite, at least not consciously. Met his tongue with a few strokes of her own. Met the last of her resistance when he tugged her fully against him at the expense of her resolve.

That will be all....That will be all....That will be—

Suddenly her back was against the door and Ash was leaning into her and she was mentally scolding her legs not to wrap around his waist. His hands came to rest on her hips and hers were at the dip of his strong spine threatening to move lower to explore his regal rearend.

His mouth was gentle yet firm against hers while his tongue made silky forays between her parted lips. His fingertips traveled in feather strokes over her bottom, up her waist, then his thumbs grazed the sides of her breasts in a maddening, circular motion.

When Ash pressed against her, Karen was well aware the sheikh had a secret weapon below the fabric of his slacks. If she didn't stop this insanity immediately, she might get to experience its potency right here, right now, on the floor near the door without ceremony. Without the *wedding* ceremony.

That will definitely be all....

But it wasn't Karen who broke the kiss. Ash did. Yet

he kept his arms securely around her as he said, ''I believe that was much more effective than a handshake.'' Then he stepped back and surveyed her from scalp to shoes.

Karen could only imagine what she looked like at that moment, probably glassy-eyed and red-lipped without the benefit of lipstick because she doubted she had any left on her lips. Several strands of her unruly hair rained down into her face, a few in her eyes. Regardless, she had no trouble seeing Ash standing there with his hands back in his pockets and the sultry smile back on his face.

Karen finger-combed her hair away, straightened her blouse and picked up her purse that had somehow landed on the floor. ''I need to go now. Thank you. I look forward to hearing from you.'' Such cold, dry departing words considering that hot, wet kiss.

His smile could stop a speeding missile. ''I certainly look forward to when we next meet, hopefully before we make our appearance at the altar.''

Karen felt like a wooden marionette with hinges instead of joints. ''We probably shouldn't see each other until the wedding.''

''Are you concerned that we might not be able to stop with only a kiss?''

Exactly. ''I'm going to be busy.''

He nodded. ''As you wish, Karen. I will keep myself busy as well until our wedding day, though I have no doubt I'll be thinking of you often. Of us. Together.''

Karen needed to get out of there and fast. She reached behind her for the door handle. ''Call me when you have the arrangements set.''

''You may depend on it.''

Karen jerked open the door and closed it behind her without giving the sheikh a second glance. But she knew deep down that in the next few days she would definitely be giving him, giving the wedding, giving his heady kisses more than a second thought.

"You may kiss your bride."

After all of Karen's anxious moments the past three days, the sleepless nights, the endless soul-searching and whirlwind planning, it had all come down to this moment. Even though they had signed a prenuptial arrangement outlining the terms of the marriage only a few hours ago, she still questioned the wisdom of agreeing to the proposal. But it was much too late to turn back now.

Karen looked from the nice lady judge to Sheikh Ashraf ibn-Saalem, her husband. *Oh, my.*

She half expected to find I've-got-you-now in Ash's expression. Instead, she saw a glimmer of hesitation in his dark eyes, her own questions reflected in his gaze as if maybe he, too, wondered if they had done the right thing.

Karen waited with nervous anticipation to seal the deal while her cousins Daniel and Maria looked on. Yet Ash only brushed her lips with an innocent kiss and gave her hand a reassuring squeeze, the same hand that now sported a gold band encrusted with multi-colored stones including several diamonds. Ash had told her it once belonged to his mother, the queen of Zhamyr. And now it was on Karen's finger, a woman who was very far removed from royalty.

Ash, on the other hand, didn't have a ring. Karen had considered buying him one until he'd allowed as how he didn't care for rings. No big deal, Karen decided. Real marriages required rings, not those with the sole goal of producing a child. If it had been more, she would have insisted Ash wear some kind of wedding band. After all, he was her husband and she would definitely want women to know that the sheikh was off the market *if* the marriage were real.

Daniel moved forward, slapped Ash on the back and said, "Welcome to the family."

Ash shook Daniel's hand. "I am most happy to be related to you if only by marriage."

Maria offered Karen the bouquet of roses that Ash had presented to Karen before the wedding. "You make a lovely bride, cousin."

Karen took the flowers and gave Maria a sympathetic look. "And you will, too, some day."

"I hope so." Maria glanced at Daniel and Ash, who were still conversing. "I need to go," she said in a hushed voice.

"Sure." Karen turned to Ash. "I'll be in the ladies' room for a few moments." At least she could be assured he wouldn't follow her and Maria in there. Or at least she thought he wouldn't. But just in case he had other ideas, she told him, "We can meet out front in a few moments."

Ash sent her a sly grin. "On the courthouse lawn?"

The rogue. The sexy, self-assured rogue. "On the steps. Standing on the steps."

Ash bowed. "As you wish, my lovely wife."

Wife. Karen wasn't sure she would ever get used to being his wife. But she was his wife, if only temporarily, and she might as well get used to it. Get used to that and the fact that tonight they would be together in every way.

As Karen followed Maria down the hallway, she shivered with anticipation when she considered making love with Ash. When she considered she might like it.

Thankfully the restroom was deserted, allowing Karen and Maria a few moments alone before Maria departed for Montana. ''Do you have the train tickets?'' Karen asked.

Maria patted her purse. ''Right here. The train leaves at 3:00 p.m. and I should arrive in Silver Valley day after tomorrow by bus. I called Louis and he said he'd be glad to pick me up. He was so nice, and I can't thank you enough.''

''Give Louis and Magdalene my love.'' Karen hugged Maria. ''Take care, okay?''

Maria swiped at her face now moist with tears. ''I will. I'll call you when I get there.''

''You do that, and stop crying.'' Karen sniffed. ''You're going to make me blubber all over my wedding dress.'' A simple white satin sheath that she'd purchased the day after she'd said yes to the sheikh—the day after she'd decided to change her life and her future by marrying a man she barely knew.

''You take care, too,'' Maria said. ''And, Karen, keep your options open, as well as your heart. You never know what might come of this union.''

''Hopefully, a baby.'' And nothing more. ''You do the same, okay?''

''I'll try,'' Maria assured her.

And so would Karen. She would try to keep an open mind. But an open heart? That seemed somewhat dangerous. As dangerous as the pleasant thought of spending hours in Ash's arms. Her husband.

Oh, wow.

Four

"I can't believe you're actually working on your wedding day, missy."

From behind the counter, Karen regarded Mimi Fazano, a five-foot, sixty-something, dynamo waitress with short-cropped gray hair who had as much earthy charm as the old-time atmosphere of the gelateria. "It was a simple courthouse ceremony. Not that big of a deal, really. Just something to make everything official." To Karen, the whole concept of being married to Ash still didn't seem official. Maybe tonight. Maybe after she was in Ash's bed, in his arms, making love with him. Procreating, she reminded herself. Making a baby, not actually making love.

Mimi shoved the cash register drawer closed with one bony hip. "You should be enjoying your honeymoon. Why, my Johnny, God rest his soul, took me to Florida after our wedding. Of course, we had to stay with his mother. Such a mama's boy, my Johnny. But I loved him dearly for over forty years.''

Karen smiled through a sudden bout of melancholy. She had so wanted to hold out for love before she married. Instead, she had entered into a daddy deal with a prince. ''It happened so quickly that we didn't have time to plan a trip.''

Mimi narrowed her brown eyes. ''You don't happen to have a little peanut in the shell? A bun in the oven? Not that I would ever pass judgment. Johnny, may he sleep with the angels, never got me pregnant. But we certainly had a fine time trying all those years.''

''No, no baby on board.'' Not yet. Maybe tonight. Maybe when she and Ash took to his bed, her with a bad case of raging hormones and him with a serious case of seductiveness. She certainly didn't need to think about that during her shift or she'd be in danger of anointing customers with gelato.

Mimi eyed her with skepticism. ''Regardless of your reasons for hurrying this wedding, you should be celebrating right now. It's not every day a woman gets married. Unless you're my poker partner, Carol Ann, who's on her fifth husband now. Or maybe it's her sixth. I've lost count. But in your case, since this is your first experience with matrimony, you should be with that young man of yours. And here you are, hard at work.''

Karen glanced around the sparsely occupied dining room. ''I'm not really doing that much at the moment.''

Mimi cackled. ''You could be if you went home to your new husband. If he's like most men, he's waiting anxiously for a nighttime ride with his bride.''

Ashraf Saalem wasn't like most men Karen had known, and that in itself was a little frightening at times. She couldn't always read him and she had to confess his air of mystery did draw her on some level. The thought of him waiting at the hotel suite for her—waiting to make love to her—caused her pulse to trip several times. If he was still speaking to her. He had been none too pleased when she'd nixed a trip out of town and hadn't arranged to take the remainder of the day off.

But with Maria now on her way to Montana, the shop would be short-staffed and Karen had promised to look after things in Maria's absence. "Mimi, you and I both know that it's going to be hectic tonight."

"That's why I've called that Veronica with the platinum hair, the one who's just a few eggs short of a carton. All that bleach must've destroyed a few brain cells. But the men certainly like her."

Karen had learned early on that Mimi thought anyone under the age of sixty qualified as a girl. "True, Veronica is a little slow. For that reason, and since Maria won't be here, I need to stay at least for a while. I promise I'll leave at eight when the mayhem dies down." By then she should be ready to join Ash. She'd be a little less nervous. After finishing the cup of cappuccino she now clutched in her hand, she should probably lay off the caffeine just to be on the safe side.

Mimi frowned. "Speaking of Maria, I'm wondering what's going on with that girl. It's not like her to take off at all much less on the day of her cousin's wedding."

"Something unexpected came up." Karen hoped Mimi dropped it for now. Eventually she would have to inform the staff that Maria wouldn't be back for a while, after she knew for certain that her cousin was settled in Montana.

"I think what's been ailing our Maria has something to do with a man," Mimi announced in her trademark crusty voice.

Karen fumbled with her cup of cappuccino, nearly spilling its contents on her white blouse. The phone rang, giving her a welcome interruption. ''Baronessa,'' she answered with a fake smile in her voice.

''I am beginning to wonder if I will ever have my wife here with me.''

Karen set the cup on the counter and white-knuckled the phone as her palms began to perspire, along with the rest of her. ''Um, it's going to be at least another few hours.''

Ash's rough sigh filtered through the line. ''That is a long time for a man to wait on his wedding day.''

''I'm sorry but it's going to get pretty uncontrollable here now that the evening crowd is beginning to arrive.''

''I would suggest that once you arrive here it could become a bit uncontrollable as well. In a very pleasant way.''

She didn't want to react to the innuendo, but Karen couldn't prevent the stream of heat mixed with chills flowing through her. At least he didn't seem angry. At least he was speaking to her, loud and clear. ''I'll be there as soon as I can get away.''

''I hope you arrive soon. The champagne is now chilling but I fear the ice is melting as we speak.''

So was Karen in response to his deep, husky voice. ''I'm not sure I should have any champagne. It makes me kind of crazy.''

''I would have no objection to you being a bit crazy. I must admit that I'm feeling somewhat that way at the moment, imagining divesting you of your clothing.''

Karen glanced over her shoulder at Mimi who pretended not to listen. ''Will that be all?''

''First I must warn you, I've already removed all of my clothing. And I've built a fire for our enjoyment.''

The image of Ash lying naked before the hearth jumped into Karen's brain like a practiced pole-vaulter. A slow, uneven breath escaped her lips. "That sounds..." *Heavenly.* "Interesting."

"Oh, I am certain it will be. More interesting than either you or I could imagine. Have I been successful in encouraging you to leave early?"

He'd encouraged Karen to fantasize about making love with him. The conception should be her only concern, but she couldn't help considering the pleasure Ash was offering. So what if she actually let go enough to enjoy the process? After all, she was a woman and he was a man—a virile, seductive, enticing man. Her libido was restless and he was offering to appease it.

Tonight, and only tonight, she would allow herself the freedom to give up a little control to gain a little satisfaction and hopefully a child. Tonight, and only tonight, she would give herself completely to the sheikh, at least from a physical standpoint. Emotionally, she would have to remain strong.

"Karen, shall I tell you what else I have imagined?"

Once more she glanced at Mimi who was grinning like mad. Karen propped a hand on the freezer case housing the gelati then immediately pulled back. If she didn't, she was in grave danger of melting every last vat of the ice cream. "That's really not ne—"

"I am greatly curious to know how your bare skin will feel to my hands. How you will taste. All of you. How you will feel surrounding me when I bring you to—"

"I've got to go now."

Karen slammed down the phone and turned at the sound of Mimi's grainy laugh.

"My, my, missy. Either that phone's on fire or you've

suddenly decided you're in a big hurry to get out of here.''

The only fire present at the moment had landed on Karen's face. Blushing, she said, ''Well, Ash probably has dinner waiting on me.'' A feast of the senses. ''I guess I really hate to disappoint him, so—''

Mimi waved a hand in dismissal. ''Get out of here. We'll handle it fine, as I'm sure you'll handle your husband fine.''

Another round of rough laughter followed Karen all the way out Baronessa's door.

All the way home, Karen gave her ovaries a pep talk. If they chose to cooperate, then she could happily get the job done tonight. If they didn't, then she would have to continue to make love with Ash a little longer.

Now why was that not such a terrible prospect? Karen knew why. During the phone call he'd had her worked up and woozy with only a few well-chosen words said in a voice that could persuade a saint to sin. Of course, he could be all talk and no action. And someone could show up on her doorstep next January and hand her a million bucks, too.

Karen arrived at the hotel in a remarkably short time considering the commuter traffic and her inability to focus on driving. In the elevator, she was grateful that the attendant kept his eyes to himself. She was strung so tight that she might have to slug him if he even looked at her crossways.

Once outside the penthouse door, Karen hesitated. What if Ash hadn't been kidding? What if he did greet her naked as the day he was born? Surely not. But if he happened to be without clothing, she would keep her eyes averted and try not to fall out in the foyer.

Drawing in a broken breath, she started to knock then remembered that Ash had given her a card key. She rummaged around in her purse—the pesky culprit that had brought her to this moment. And it couldn't even accommodate her enough to cough up the key.

When Karen finally found it, she slipped the card into the lock with trembling fingers and opened the door to find the suite starkly silent and completely dark except for the warm glow of firelight radiating from the small hearth in the sitting area.

Karen visually searched the room, her gaze coming to rest on the plush chair facing the door, a chair containing her new husband. Her naked new husband.

Obviously he was a man of his word, Karen decided. A man with a body that could melt a midwinter Montana snowfall.

Her eyes immediately homed in on his bare chest revealing smooth bronzed skin stretched tight over his pecs, the territory interrupted only by a fine smattering of dark hair that spanned the space between his collarbones. Below that, a ribbon of masculine hair traveled to his navel. Below that…

Karen didn't dare look any farther but that was exactly what she did while trying to breathe with some semblance of normality. He sat with his legs stretched out before him, crossed at the ankles, a champagne flute balanced in one hand and an expression that told her he was somewhat amused over her inability to tear her eyes away. He seemed as comfortable with his nudity as Karen was uncomfortable with it.

Karen wasn't altogether uncomfortable; she was fascinated. Fascinated by the sensual image he presented. Fascinated that he was already fully aroused. Normally she was a butt connoisseur but considering Ash's ample attributes, she had no doubt that he could handle the conception quite well. But could she?

Tossing her overnight bag onto the adjacent sofa, Karen headed toward the bathroom muttering, "I need a shower." She needed a tank of oxygen.

As she passed him, Ash caught her wrist. "I will have the champagne poured for you on your return."

She didn't look at him for fear she might forgo the shower. "Good. And do you mind putting something on?"

"Music?"

"Clothes."

"If that is what you wish. I'll have on my robe when you rejoin me."

"Good."

"And I look forward to having you remove it."

So did Karen. "I'll be back in a few minutes."

In the bedroom, Karen closed the door and collapsed her boneless body against it. She hugged her arms to her chest to stop the shivers, but it didn't work. She wasn't sure her legs would work, either, but she had to move. She had to bathe and prepare for the conception. Prepare for whatever Ash had planned for her tonight. As if she could really prepare for that.

Ash could not imagine what was taking Karen so long in the bath. He supposed it was possible that she was anxious. Perhaps he had inadvertently shocked her with his nudity, though he had given her fair warning. Perhaps he should remember that they were unfamiliar with each other. He would take care of that soon, if she ever returned.

In reality, he was experiencing some unease despite the fact that seeing Karen come through his door, even fully clothed, had served to fuel his desire for her. Created a need so strong that the force of it had taken him aback.

Ash paced the length of the room while he considered the reasons behind his own disquiet. Normally, he had no qualms whatsoever when it came to making love. He had learned at a relatively young age to pleasure a woman and take his own pleasure from the act. He had been groomed by the best, a beautiful woman five years his senior who had been uninhibited and an excellent teacher. He had always thought fondly of her, and through the years, he had practiced what she had so skillfully taught him.

Tonight his concern centered on only one woman—his wife. He worried he might not be able to break down Karen's resistance so she would allow herself to take without hesitation what he offered. He worried that perhaps she would only view the consummation as a means to an end, that she would see him as being no better than a stallion providing breeding services. He longed to have her know him as a man, not as a prince. A man who very much wanted her, all of her, including her trust and her respect.

That was very important to him, and something he had not desired from a woman in many years. Fifteen years, to be exact. But he would not think about that tonight. He would turn all his energy to Karen and her needs. He would utilize every method he had learned and some he had discovered through experimentation, and there were many in his repertoire.

First, he would remember to maintain control, take his time, go slowly….

"Ash?"

He turned to find Karen dressed in a flowing, sheer

lace gown the color of a desert rose that revealed the shadowed curves of her body, her light brown hair framing her face in soft waves.

The vision of Karen standing there backlit by the fire, and the knowledge that she was his, at least for tonight, caused Ash to grow hard as slate beneath the robe he now wore, every muscle in his body growing taut from a need to take her right where she now stood.

But when he saw the hesitancy in her eyes, he remembered that he needed to pace himself, stay in control, rely on gentle persuasion and not the desperation for release that his body demanded. ''Come with me,'' he said as he held out his hand to her.

She moved slowly toward him and took his hand. When he guided her to the sofa and pulled her down to his side, she frowned. ''What's wrong with the bedroom?''

He poured her a glass of champagne from the bottle set in the silver bucket resting on the coffee table before them. ''The bedroom will come later. Perhaps we should talk first.''

He offered her the flute and noticed her hands trembled as she took it from him. Ash experienced a slight tremor as well, but it had nothing to do with stress. The faint outline of her nipples exposed through the gossamer lace covering her round breasts, the dark shading at the apex of her thighs, engaged him in the ultimate battle for control.

She stared at the champagne, rimming a slender finger round and round the edge of the glass. ''What do you want to talk about?''

What I am going to do to you, with you. ''Your day.'' He shifted slightly, keeping a comfortable distance between them in order to keep his desire temporarily at bay.

"Would you like something to eat? I can have room service deliver a tray."

"No. I grabbed a burger this afternoon."

"Are you sure you would not like something that will help you maintain your strength?"

"Why would I need any strength?"

"Because I intend to preoccupy you until the early hours of the morning."

Color rose high in her cheeks, a few shades lighter than the negligee. "Oh." She twirled a lock of hair around one slender finger, sparking Ash's imagination. "I'm okay. I had an order of fries, too."

Ash placed his champagne on the table and draped one arm casually along the back of the sofa. "You seem tired."

She took a sip of the wine then clutched the glass to her breasts. "I am. It was a long day."

Ash suddenly wished he were the champagne flute. "Yes, it was. A very long, hard day." Coming upon an idea that might make her more at ease, he took the glass from her and set it next to his. "Lie back."

"Ash—"

"I only want to help you relax."

With wariness calling out from eyes that appeared golden in the firelight, she stretched out with her head resting on the sofa's arm, her arms folded beneath her breasts. Ash brought her legs across his lap, taking care not to come near his burgeoning erection. The slightest bit of contact in that area would make him forget his vow of patience.

He began his ministrations with her feet, delicate feet with toenails painted the color of her red gown. He worked her instep, her heels, those delicate toes that he found very intriguing. When he moved his massage up to her calves, she tensed and he realized that he would have another battle on his hands to make her relax. Continued conversation might aid in his cause to distract her as he worked his way to his destination.

"Where was Maria off to in such a hurry today?" he asked.

Karen closed her eyes. "She had somewhere she had to be."

"Baronessa?"

"No."

He slipped his hand to the inside of Karen's knee and waited for her reaction. When she remained still, keeping her eyes closed, he continued his gentle stroking and the conversation. "I find it odd that she would leave knowing you were recently wed."

"She needed a vacation."

"Does this mean she will not be returning for a while?"

"I'm not sure how long she'll be gone."

"Where did she go?"

She sighed. "Montana. And her location has to remain a secret. You can't tell anyone, not even Daniel."

Ash found that to be surprising news, Maria traveling to the state where Karen once resided. He also found it odd that she obviously was in hiding. But that Karen trusted him enough to take him into her confidence pleased him. "I assure you I will tell no one. Yet I am wondering what business she has in Montana."

"No business. Just a break. That's all I'm at liberty to say at this time."

Ash thought of several ways he could make her talk yet he wasn't in the mood for more conversation. He slipped his fingertips to the inside of her thighs and Karen's eyes snapped open.

"Are you feeling more relaxed?" he asked as he continued caressing her leg with tempered movements.

"Not exactly."

"Tell me what I might do to assist you."

She released a slow, strained breath when he moved his fingertips up a fraction. "You're doing okay."

Okay? That did not set well with Ash. Determination drove him from the sofa and onto his knees beside her. Her lips, like her toes, were painted a deep crimson. Very tempting, but he wasn't ready to kiss her yet. At least not there.

"What are we doing now?" she asked, her voice as uneasy as her eyes.

"*You* are to remain where you are and enjoy." He lowered one thin strap and whisked his lips over her bare shoulder, then proceeded to do the same with the other strap. He could feel her heart thrumming where his chest pressed against her breasts and he knew that he was somewhat successful with his seduction.

"You are very beautiful," he murmured as he massaged her bare shoulders. "Are you relaxed yet?"

She hid a yawn behind her hand. "I'm definitely getting there. You're doing fine."

At least his efforts had been elevated from "okay" to "fine." He vowed to arrive at "wonderfully" soon. He pledged to give her the gratification she deserved, to prove to her that meeting her needs meant more than meeting his own. But not yet, not until he knew she was completely ready for him. Until he knew he had her full attention.

When Ash moved to the end of the sofa, Karen sent him a confused look. "Why did you stop?"

He pulled her up to his side, brought his arm around

her and nudged her head against his shoulder. "You should rest."

"Rest?"

He whisked a kiss across her forehead and stroked her hair. "You're tired from your day."

"I'm fine, really." She yawned again.

"Are you certain?"

"It's the champagne."

"You've had only a few sips."

"I told you it makes me crazy."

He leaned forward, slid the champagne glass from the table and held it to her lips. "You should have more then."

Smiling, she took another drink then ran her tongue over her lips, stirring Ash's body. "This is very good. French?"

He considered licking the moisture at the corner of her mouth but with great effort restrained himself. Unfortunately, one part of his body showed no sign of restraint. "Yes, it's French. The best."

"Of course. What else but the finest things for a prince?"

Ash had hoped that she would forget his status and see him only as her prospective lover. "Tonight I am simply a man. A man in the company of a beautiful woman who happens to be his wife."

"I never had any doubt about your manliness." She sent a pointed look at the obvious ridge beneath his robe.

"I will be more than happy to remove all your doubts and allow you to remove this robe to uncover the proof." She reached for the robe's sash and he stopped her with a hand on her wrist. "After you rest awhile."

"I'm honestly not that tired."

Nor was Ash, but he was determined. "Why the hurry?

Would you not prefer us to proceed at a leisurely pace? Or would you prefer hard and fast?''

''Yes. I mean no.'' She glanced away. ''Leisurely is fine, I guess.''

Ash smiled to himself as he offered her another sip of champagne that she gladly took. Obviously there was a side of Karen he had yet to uncover, a sensual facet that longed for wild, uninhibited lovemaking. He looked forward to accommodating her at some point in time. Tonight he chose to savor each moment.

After Ash set the glass aside and twined their fingers together, Karen studied their joined hands. ''Very large,'' she murmured.

''Large?''

''Your hands. They're big. But then you're kind of big…all over.''

''Does that concern you?''

''Not really.''

''Good. Now lay your head back on my shoulder and close your eyes for a while.''

''But what about the baby?''

As suspected, creating a child was still her principal plan. Ash's plan involved taking her attention off the conception and onto the process of achieving that goal. ''We have all night to learn each other. Right now you need to relax. I prefer you awake and energized before we go any further.''

She settled back against him. ''Okay, if you insist.'' Her head snapped up again. ''But I'm not going to sleep.''

Yet it wasn't long before Karen's steady breathing echoed in the silent room and Ash realized she was indeed asleep. He had wanted her to relax, perhaps not quite that much, but as he'd said, there were still many hours left in the night.

If he had his way, they would come together every night for the rest of his days. But unless he could convince Karen to allow him to touch her after she conceived, to stay with him long after their child was born, these few moments might be all he ever had. He intended to make the most of them.

Time was on his side. For now.

Five

Karen had no concept of time or place, only that she was in a bed and she had no idea how she'd gotten there. Once she came fully awake, she glanced to her right at the green glow of the nearby clock that read half-past midnight. She looked to her left to see a figure stretched out beside her.

Ashraf Saalem. Her husband. Naked again.

The break in the heavy curtains allowed streamers of light coming from the Boston skyline to fall over him as he lay on his belly, his arms crossed above his head on the pillow, his face turned toward the window. Karen rolled to her side and studied the rise and fall of his strong back, the strength of his spine and the taut curve of his buttocks.

He was a magnificent man and he was hers for the taking. Or so she'd thought. She had wanted him to make love to her on the sofa, had almost begged him to continue, but her pride had prevented her from doing so. Yes, she had been tired, more than she'd realized. But not so exhausted that she wouldn't have gladly let him continue. Yet she had felt very secure curled up at his side, with his arm wrapped around her and her head against his shoulder. So relaxed that in only a matter of minutes, she had fallen asleep. And somehow he had carried her into the room without her notice. What else had he done?

Karen patted her chest and realized her gown was still intact. So was her need for him. Her need to create a child, she corrected. After all, that was why she was here, to make a baby.

On that thought, Karen reached out her hand to touch him then pulled back. For some reason she was afraid to rouse him, to unleash the power she inherently knew he possessed. A shudder ran through her, not from fear but from excitement, from the notion that this could be more than she could handle, making love with Ash.

As concerns whirled around in her head, Karen's hand moved to his back where she pressed a palm between his shoulder blades. His body temperature was volcanic, not surprising at all. Everything about him reminded her of fire, able to consume a woman's good sense in a matter of moments.

He didn't stir at all, even when she sent a fingertip down the track of his spine to the dip immediately below his waist. She couldn't stop there. Oh, no, not when faced with the tempting prospect of testing the firmness of his butt. She ran her palm over that masculine terrain, then on to the back of his hair-covered thighs, then back up again.

She felt like a child discovering clay for the first time, felt like a woman in dire need as she explored with abandon, tracing a fingertip lightly along the cleft, stopping right where his thighs came together. Karen squeezed her own thighs tightly against the onslaught of damp heat when she considered going farther in her journey.

She wanted him. Oh, how she wanted him. She wanted to know how it would feel to have him turn her into a mass of mindless feminine need.

Funny that Carl should enter her mind at that moment. She'd never wanted him with the same desperation. But then Carl's idea of lovemaking had entailed a once-a-week session whether needed or not. Afterward, Karen had always felt somewhat used, cheated, unsatisfied, and she hadn't known how to tell him. He hadn't asked, either.

Forcing her ex-fiancé from her mind, Karen turned her focus solely on her new husband. With a good deal of bravado, she inched closer to him and rested her lips against his back. Even if she didn't wake him, she would definitely enjoy her exploration.

"I see you're awake now."

Karen rolled away to find Ash had turned his face toward her. "So are you." Obviously, dummy.

A laugh rumbled low in his chest. "I have yet to sleep."

"But—" Karen couldn't think of one thing to say. He had known all along what she was doing. Maybe that should have embarrassed her, but for some reason it didn't. It gave her an odd sense of power.

"Are you feeling more refreshed?" he asked.

She was feeling hot and bothered. "Yes."

He worked his way to his side, facing her. "Refreshed enough to continue with our honeymoon?"

Oh, yeah. "If you're not too tired now."

He ran a slow finger down the cleft of her breasts. "I have never felt more animated in my life."

When he moved over her, Karen's breath caught in her chest. He reached for the bedside lamp and snapped it on, completely illuminating the room. "What are you doing?" she asked in a scratchy voice.

He hovered above her, his thick dark hair unkempt and incredibly sexy, his dark eyes roaming leisurely over her body. "I want to see you. All of you."

Karen could see all of him—almost. She could see the width of his sculpted chest, the flat plane of his belly, but she couldn't see anything below that. She could feel him, though. Could feel his "secret weapon" pressing against her hip and she wouldn't be a bit surprised if she spontaneously combusted at any given moment.

"Take off your gown," he said in a low, lusty voice.

"Don't you want to do it?"

"I would gladly do it, but I would prefer to watch you undress for me."

Karen didn't have one whit of will left to protest. When she started to slip her arms out of the straps, Ash commanded, "Stand by the bed."

Stand? She wasn't sure she could. "Why?"

"It would give me pleasure to watch the material fall away from your body. I believe you will enjoy it as well."

Karen wasn't so sure about that. She'd never undressed for a man before, not even Carl who preferred darkness. She had never really seen Carl naked in the light.

But if she did what Ash had requested, she would definitely be able to see every fabulous part of him and that drove her out of the bed.

She tossed back the covers from her lower body and slid off the mattress to stand on jelly legs. Ash remained on his side, his elbow bent and his jaw braced on his palm, his near-black eyes trained on her face.

Forcing her gaze to remain locked on his, Karen slipped her arms from the straps then tugged the bodice down, baring her breasts. A cool draft of air flowed over her and that, combined with the heat in Ash's eyes, caused her flesh to pebble.

Only then did she venture a glance below Ash's waist to garner his true reaction. A very observable reaction. And as she slowly slid the gown down, she experienced a heady sense of control as she watched him grow and swell right before her eyes. She paused when she had the fabric worked below her abdomen, hesitated to increase the tension. Not that Ash looked the least bit tense, at least not his face. Had it not been for his current state of arousal, it would seem that this was an everyday occurrence for him. Maybe it was.

Karen refused to ponder how many women he had asked to do this for him. She only considered that she was doing it for him now, and that he was, for all intents and purposes, her husband, even if not in the truest sense of the word.

She managed a smile as she shimmied the gown from her hips. It fell in a pool of lace at her feet and she stepped over it, bringing her closer to the bed.

Ash sat up, draped his legs over the side of the bed and perched on the edge to face her. While Karen stood there fighting chills and heat, he visually scanned her body.

"Do you approve?" she asked.

He brought his gaze back to her eyes. "Come closer and I will show you how much I approve."

She moved forward and came to a stop immediately before him. He parted his legs and pulled her between them. With a gentle fingertip, he traced a circular path around one breast then the other. "Very beautiful," he murmured.

When he flicked his tongue over one nipple, then the other, Karen swayed forward in offering. He suckled her and she felt the steady pull all the way to her womb and lower.

He kept his hands braced on her waist while she propped her hands on his shoulders to keep from toppling over. Then he took his mouth away. Karen wanted to groan from the loss of sensation, but not for long as he kneaded her bottom much the same as she had his. "You feel very good." He explored and fondled her buttocks, with each pass coming nearer to the point between her legs where she needed his attention the most.

He brought his hands around to her hips and stroked her pelvis all the while watching her. When he finally made it to the layer of curls, an almost pleading sound climbed up Karen's throat and came out of her mouth despite her attempts to stop it. Never had she been so close to begging someone to soothe the ache. Never had she been so close to coming apart.

"Do you wish me to touch you, Karen?"

"Yes," she said on a breathy sigh.

"Then I shall and you will watch."

And she did watch him, watched as he parted her flesh. Watched as he made maddening passes over and around her tender, aching center, first lightly, then more insistent, then lightly again, almost teasing her into total oblivion. "You are beautiful here, too," he said, his gaze leveled on the place he now touched.

Karen was lost in the eroticism of the moment as he caressed her with a proficiency she had only fantasized about until now. Her knees almost buckled, and had it not been for her grip on his shoulders, she might have fallen. But that didn't stop Ash's carnal assault on her senses or the threatening climax building and building in Karen.

Then he took his hands away. This time Karen groaned, or more like moaned. Was he determined to drive her insane? If he told her she needed to rest, she'd have to sock him.

"I'm not finished," he assured her. "I simply want to feel you when you reach your climax." He took her hands into his and tugged her forward. "Come to me now."

Karen straddled his thighs and, with his help, lowered herself onto him in slow increments. Before she could attempt to take all of him inside her, Ash stopped her with a solid grip on her waist. "Relax for a moment."

Relax? How could she relax? Not in this position. And why was he so intent on her relaxing? "I'm fine," she insisted.

"You will be better in a moment." Keeping one hand on her waist, he touched her with the other, stroked her without mercy until he brought her back to that place where nothing mattered but sheer sensation. The orgasm hit her in strong, mind-bending jolts.

This time Ash groaned and muttered something she didn't understand but it sounded almost desperate, followed by "Do with me what you will. You are in control now."

"My pleasure."

And it was. The ultimate pleasure. All thoughts of the purpose of this union left Karen's mind as she immersed herself in the moment. With Ash's hands planted firmly on her hips, she moved in a rhythm that began slowly before growing wild and reckless.

She kissed Ash with all the passion bubbling inside

her, tangled her tongue with his in frantic forays not unlike the love they now made. Karen was consumed by a power she couldn't comprehend when Ash broke the kiss and in a harsh voice said, *"Now."*

With that, he pushed her hips down until he was deeper inside her, deeper than Karen ever thought possible. His chest heaved against her breasts and his body tensed. She felt the pulse of his climax from the inside out, felt him shudder with the force of it.

Ash collapsed onto his back, bringing Karen down with him. He continued to tremble, or maybe she was trembling; Karen couldn't tell since they were so closely joined. His heart beat in an erratic rhythm against her cheek while hers fluttered in her chest.

They stayed that way for a time, silent, until Ash rolled her over and rose above her. She expected him to say something but instead he kissed her, a languid, gentle, honeyed kiss that contrasted with their uncontrolled love-making. A tender kiss that spoke to Karen on a level she didn't want to acknowledge.

Ash moved up onto the bed, taking her with him to share his pillow as they faced each other. He enfolded her in his strong arms, stroked her hair, made her feel protected and appreciated for the first time in a long time. Had she ever felt this way before? No, and that frightened her.

Ash spoke to her in whispers, concerned that he had been too forceful. She assured him he had been wonderful, and that made him smile, a smile as soft as his continuing kisses. A fissure of emotion opened in Karen's heart, one she had been so determined to keep closed. She told herself that it was only an illusion, that what she now felt for Ash was a product of incredible sex. Told her heart to stay strong, stay protected.

They remained that way for a long time, holding each other in the quiet aftermath, Karen savoring his arms surrounding her. Then he slipped one hair-roughened thigh between her legs and rubbed intimately against her. The dam broke again, the sensations came calling again, and Karen opened herself to him again. He entered her with a slow steady glide, caressed her with capable fingers until she was lost to everything, lost to him. Lost to a moment where she started to believe that this mysterious man who filled her body so completely could easily fill the void in her soul.

Ash collapsed heavily against her, but she didn't find the weight a burden at all. She reveled in it, reveled in the feel of him, the roughness of his jaw against her cheek, his warm, ragged breath playing over her neck where he had buried his face. Much sooner than she would have liked, he moved from atop her but kept his arm resting across her abdomen and his cheek against her cheek. When she heard the sound of his steady breathing and knew that he slept, only then did reality take hold.

She had given him everything tonight in hopes of creating a child and in turn, when she'd taken him inside her body, he'd threatened to enter her heart. She couldn't allow that to happen. She couldn't give up a good deal of her soul to another man for fear that he might want it all.

This one night with Ash would have to be enough. But deep down she worried it never would be.

Shortly before dawn, Ash walked onto the balcony with a cup of coffee and feelings he could not explain.

He had correctly assumed that making love with Karen would be a most pleasurable experience, and it had been that and more. But he had not bargained for the odd heaviness in his heart after they had made love, a heaviness that still existed. It went far beyond desire and called up a wariness from deep within his soul.

He did not fear many things. He had braved the steep slopes of mountains, conquered the vast, unpredictable spectrum of investing, disentangled himself from his father's hold and left the only home he had ever known to pursue his own path in the world. Falling in love with another woman—a woman who might leave him as well—was something he dare not encounter. He could not allow himself anything beyond warm feelings for her. He could not want more from her, or from himself.

His obligation to Karen should be based solely on creating a child and establishing a relationship built on mutual respect, not love. He had learned to shield himself against succumbing to those emotions, yet in one night Karen had exposed him in a way no other woman had in fifteen years. He would be damned if he gave into that weakness.

Granted, he did crave her passion, appreciated her strength and wanted her with every breath that he took. Even the cool Boston breeze did nothing to quell the heat when he considering rejoining her in bed to reach even greater heights. He had not even begun to show her all the ways a man and woman could take pleasure in each other. He preferred to reveal those aspects a little at a time. If she decided to allow him that honor in the coming months. The coming years.

"I'm leaving now."

Ash turned to see Karen standing in the doorway dressed in a white tailored shirt and black skirt, her hair pulled back into a plait. Unless he was mistaken, she looked ready to return to work, and that infuriated him.

Carefully he set his cup of espresso down on the patio

table and with effort kept a tight rein on his temper. "Where are you off to so early in the morning?"

"Work. I have to open up since Maria won't be there."

"People actually prefer ice cream for breakfast?"

"You'd be surprised but no, most come in for pastries and coffee. We have quite a few regular customers who show up every morning when we open at seven."

Ash fisted his hands into the pockets of his robe. "I assume you will be off earlier today due to your morning arrival?"

"Actually, I'm not sure. I need to see who's on the schedule. I'll probably have to stay until tonight."

"And after that?"

She frowned. "What do you mean?"

"Will you join me here?"

She threaded her bottom lip between her teeth. "I guess I could, at least for another couple of nights. My fertile cycle won't be over until then."

Ash took another step, anger steeping inside him. "Then you have no intention of us living together as man and wife?"

"I don't know. I mean, I love my apartment and I can't imagine you would be happy living there."

"I would be happy living wherever you might be."

Her gaze wavered. "Maybe we should discuss it later. If I don't leave now, I won't beat the traffic and I'll be late. I promised Maria I would look after things in her absence."

She had promised Ash nothing beyond being the mother of his child and that thought angered him more. "When Maria returns, it will not be necessary for you to remain employed."

Her mouth opened then fell closed. "Ash, I intend to continue working at Baronessa. I love my job."

"And if you become pregnant?"

"I can work up until a few weeks before the baby's born."

"I have no say in the matter?"

"No, you don't. I enjoy my independence. I will not stay home and do nothing. If there is a baby, I'll consider my options then."

Ash was caught between fury and frustration. Desire and determination. The fire in Karen's eyes fueled an illogical need to sweep her up into his arms and take her back to bed to use every sensual tactic he knew to make her forget work, forget everything but him.

With a strength he didn't know he possessed, he simply said, "You may return to your job now. We will discuss this and our living arrangements later."

She sent him an acrimonious look. "Thank you so much for your permission, but in terms of my job there's really nothing more to discuss."

Changing strategy, he sent her a smile. "Could I perhaps persuade you into kissing me goodbye? Something that will carry me through the day until we are together tonight?"

She sighed. "Oh, all right. I guess one little goodbye peck would be okay, although I'm not feeling very affectionate toward you at the moment."

Something Ash was determined to remedy. He strode toward her and without the slightest pause, claimed her mouth with the force of his anger, his desire. And Karen responded as she had the day she'd agreed to his proposal, as she had last night, as if she were trying to prove exactly who was in control. Ash was beginning to wonder about that very thing.

Their mouths sealed together as if each breath they drew depended on the other. Karen's bag dropped to the cement floor and her arms came around his neck. Ash circled her waist, cupped her buttocks, pulled her against him to let her know that he could easily take this further, take her beyond the limits.

Karen didn't allow anything beyond the kiss and pulled away. She picked up the bag and sent him a playful smile. "Hold that thought until tonight."

He would rather hold her. "You would leave me now in such a predicament?"

Her gaze came to rest on his predicament. "Go take a cold shower."

"That, my dear wife, is a total fallacy. Cold water does not provide relief."

She shrugged. "Well, you probably need some time to rebuild your stamina after last night anyway."

"I would not wager on that, and neither should you."

She smoothed a slender hand over her blouse. "In the meantime, order some orange juice. It's supposed to aid in fertility. I'll see you later."

With that she was gone, leaving Ash with his discomfort and a strong determination.

They had much to learn about each other, and much to decide. He refused to consider living apart from her. After all, he was her husband. Of course, the penthouse had been anything but a real home to him, except last night when Karen had been in his bed, in his arms. But this hotel room was only temporary, as it had been with all the places he had occupied over the past few years. He considered moving to Karen's current residence. An apartment would not do if they had a child, which left only one option.

Fueled by his goal, Ash made his way back into the suite and picked up the phone. If good fortune chose to be gracious, the living arrangements would be decided today.

Six

"You must come with me now."

Karen looked up from the booth where she'd been taking an order to find Ash standing beside her. He wore a black business suit, a white Arabian headdress covering his dark hair and an expression that said he meant business. "What are you doing here?"

"I am in need of your immediate assistance."

Was he expecting a nooner? "I can't just up and leave."

"Oh, yes you can, honey," said the lady with flaming red hair and equally red lips seated at the booth. "If a hunky stranger came in demanding my assistance, I'd leave in a minute."

Karen fought the little nip of pride. "He's not a stranger."

"I'm her husband," Ash said. "We were married yesterday."

The lady's eyes widened as she leveled her gaze on Karen. "And you're at work?"

Ash gave her a winning smile. "My point exactly. I've told her that we could be sunning ourselves on a private beach in the Mediterranean were she not so devoted to her job."

The redhead released a grating chuckle. "Hell, honey, if my order's holding you up, I'll get my own ice cream."

Feeling trapped, feeling like an idiot, Karen gritted her teeth and aimed her scowl on Ash. "Now you know, *dear,* I have to work in order to keep you in your designer clothes."

Ash seemed unaffected by the lie. "I would prefer you keep me out of my clothes."

The lady let go a round of strident laughter, drawing Mimi from across the room to the booth to ask, "Is there a problem over here?"

Ash extended his hand to Mimi. "I believe we have not officially met. I am Sheikh Ashraf Saalem, Karen's husband."

"Oh, yes, I remember you." Mimi shook Ash's hand and fairly blushed. "My, my, you are quite a specimen. My Johnny, God save his soul, was about as handsome as you, but not quite as tall. Are you here to see your wife?"

Ash slipped his arm around Karen's waist. "I need to steal her away for a time."

"By all means, take her," Mimi said.

Feeling totally outnumbered, Karen told Mimi, "I can't leave now, not during the lunch rush."

"Of course you can, missy. We've got plenty of people to cover for you. Now run along and take care of your husband. We can handle it without you."

Karen wanted to take care of Ash, all right. She wanted

to remove her apron and stuff it into his sexy mouth. Instead, she handed Mimi the pad and released a frustrated sigh. ''Okay, but I'll be back soon.''

The redhead laughed again. ''Take your time, honey. Rome wasn't made in a day. Neither is good lovin'.''

Karen untied her apron and tossed it underneath the counter. After grabbing her purse, she headed out the door muttering, ''This better be good.''

''I assure you it will be,'' Ash said from behind her.

Karen stopped in the middle of the sidewalk. She had no idea where they were going or if Ash had even come in a car, though she doubted he'd used public transportation.

Ash gestured toward a silver sedan parked at the curb. A Rolls-Royce. A convertible Rolls-Royce with the top down. Figures, Karen thought. Only the best.

Ash opened the door for her and she slipped inside to settle into the soft seat. Had she not been so put out over the interruption, she might have enjoyed the luxurious feel of the leather.

When Ash seated himself behind the wheel, she sent him a hard look. ''Do you mind telling me where we're going? And it better not be back to the hotel for a quickie.'' Karen experienced an unwanted thrill thinking about that prospect. Darn his sexy sheikh self.

''I have something I want to show you,'' he said.

She rolled her eyes. ''I've already seen it, Ash.''

He turned on the ignition and the car purred to life and so did Karen when he smiled. ''Although having you examine 'it' again is a pleasant thought, that is not my goal.'' He sent her a sultry glance. ''At least not at the moment.''

Now why was she so disappointed? ''Then exactly what is your goal?''

He pulled into traffic before saying, "It's a surprise, one I think will please you."

Karen couldn't imagine what else he could possibly do to please her. He had done it all last night. "I don't necessarily like surprises."

"You will like this one."

Karen resigned herself to the fact that Ash wasn't going to give an inch, at least not at the moment, and sat back to enjoy the feel of the wind on her face, thankful she'd braided her hair that morning. If not, she would probably resemble Medusa before they reached their destination.

After leaving Boston proper, they traveled along a winding highway that skirted the shoreline in places, revealing a crescent beach covered in golden sand, the water beyond it a sage green. Karen could certainly appreciate the view considering she hadn't really experienced the sea's beauty before coming to Boston. But the stately historic houses to Karen's left that faced the ocean captured her attention the most.

She commented to Ash about their magnificence and he only smiled. Obviously he had no appreciation for the historical significance of the area.

Forty minutes later, Ash passed through the Marblehead area and drove up a winding hedge-lined drive leading to a house—a beige Colonial-style, two-story house surrounded by elm and birch trees with a stand of sugar maple set out near the edge of the property. She could envision the kaleidoscope of color when the foliage began to change with the season in a matter of weeks. Right now the verdant lawns were plush and pristine, the rows of hedges neatly manicured. Yet the cracked and peeling brown paint on the trim around the dormers told her the house hadn't faired as well. But the twelve-paned windows and the double chimneys captured Karen's imagination and prompted her fantasy of living in such an elegant home. "This place is unbelievable. But what are we doing here?"

Ash put the car in park and shut off the ignition. "You will soon see."

Before Karen could ask more questions, Ash rushed around to open the door for her. She left the car and inhaled the tangy scent of sea air coming from the harbor that served as a backdrop to the estate.

Karen followed Ash up the rock walkway and when he reached the heavy entry doors, she asked, "Who lives here?"

Ash fished a key from his pocket. "We will."

Stunned, Karen searched for some appropriate retort until she followed him inside to a breathtaking foyer that would make even the most stoic person take immediate notice. The ceilings had to be at least twenty feet high, and a wide staircase covered in a faded blue carpet climbed to the upper floors. Overcome with curiosity, she walked to the bottom of the stairs, crouched down and lifted a corner of the carpet. As she suspected, the rug hid the original flooring, most likely wide board pine that had been pegged with wood, not nails.

As usual, she slipped into designer mode and immediately saw the possibilities. The entry walls were in need of a good coat of paint and she figured the rest of the house's interior would as well. A nice, patterned wallpaper here and there would definitely restore its original charm and—

Wait a minute, Karen thought as she took a mental step back. Had she actually heard Ash correctly? Did this incredible place belong to him?

Karen straightened and turned to Ash who looked very

pleased at the moment. ''I could've sworn you told me that you didn't own a home.''

''I do as of this morning.''

''Excuse me?''

''I purchased the house this morning.''

''Just like that? You went out and got a loan—''

''I paid with cash.''

Of course he had. ''Let me get this straight. You got up, had your coffee, took a shower then went wandering up the Massachusetts coastline until you came upon this house?''

He leaned against the banister. ''Actually, I spoke with Daniel this morning and when I told him what I intended to do, he suggested this place. It was built in the 1800s and used mainly as a summerhouse. Unfortunately its been tied up in an estate dispute for years, the reason for its current disrepair. I immediately saw its potential.''

So did she, darn it. ''It's very nice.'' A designer's dream kind of nice.

''The paperwork will not be finalized for a few days,'' Ash continued. ''As far as I am concerned, it is now ours.''

Ours? Marrying Ash was one thing. Having a baby with Ash was another. But owning a home with him? That sounded much more like a real marriage than Karen was prepared to deal with at the moment. ''You just took it upon yourself to buy a house for us to live in without consulting me?''

''Had you not been so determined to work, I would have consulted you. Daniel told me of your background in interior design and I believed you would be happy to decorate it as you saw fit.''

And he had seen fit to buy a house without her input. ''It definitely needs work.'' Karen walked to the banister where Ash now stood and scratched the surface with a thumbnail. "Someone painted over the mahogany. They've covered the original flooring. This house should be restored to its original state."

"And I trust it will with your vision."

Karen turned back to Ash, trying desperately to ignore how much she would cherish making this house all that it could be. "It would take money. A lot of money and a lot of time."

"Money is not an issue, and neither is time. I'm certain there are craftsmen in Boston who would do the restoration justice. Daniel is now researching those for me."

Good old Daniel, Karen thought. She had a few things to say to him, too. But she really couldn't blame her cousin. As far as Daniel knew, Karen and Ash were living in wedded bliss, planning a future together. A house was simply the next step. A gorgeous house that could be made even better.

Karen could already imagine the details. Imagine what it would be like if she were given free rein. Even if Ash hadn't provided her the opportunity to stamp her seal of approval before he bought the place, at least she could maintain some control over what was done with it from this point forward. "I would want to oversee everything."

Ash smiled. "I had hoped you would. Shall we see the rest of the house?"

Oh, no. Until Karen got some things straight, she refused to fall completely in love with this place any more than she dared fall in love with him knowing that by doing so she could face certain emotional peril. "First, I want to know what's going to happen to this house after we're no longer together."

Ash's expression turned hard, unforgiving. "You mean after the *divorce?*"

She flinched over his sudden ire. "That's exactly what I mean."

His eyes narrowed and went almost black. "It would be yours. I have no use for a house if I have no family with which to share it."

Karen felt suddenly remorseful over her lack of consideration when she saw the hurt in Ash's eyes, heard it in his tone. He had provided a home, a beautiful home, for her and their child. The least she could do was thank him then worry about the rest later. "I'm sorry, Ash. Really, it's wonderful. I only wish you would have talked to me about it first."

"And how was I to do that when you were so intent on going to work?" He folded his arms across his chest, looking powerful and no less angry. "I believed this would solve our living arrangements. There are four bedrooms on the second floor, one we will set up for our child, and one I plan to use as my office. It will be up to you to decide what will be done with the others."

"We can discuss that later." Karen automatically held out her hand. Nothing more than a friendly action, she told herself, even though she'd recently discovered that touching Ash was just this side of heaven. "Can you show me the rest of the house now?"

He gestured toward the entry opening to another room but failed to take her hand. "After you."

Karen fought the knifelike pain that impaled her heart over his refusal to touch her. She couldn't really blame him. He was only being considerate and she had carelessly ruined the moment by bringing up the whole divorce issue. But she was too afraid to hope that their marriage could be permanent. Too afraid to believe that she wouldn't eventually drown in Ash's need to stay in control of his life, their decisions. She had to remain adamant even though every time she was near him her heart executed a little tumble and she found herself wishing that they had a marriage based on more than an agreement. But they didn't.

Karen followed Ash through the adjacent living room, bare except for a white brick fireplace in the corner, and into a small hallway where he opened the door to a room with twelve-foot ceilings and muted gray walls with contrasting white molding. A dusty teardrop chandelier hung above her and dull hardwood floors creaked beneath her feet.

Considering the size of the area, Karen assumed it to be a formal parlor or dining room, albeit a large one, until Ash announced, "This is the master suite."

Karen turned to Ash, her eyes wide. "A bedroom? It's huge."

He allowed a slight smile to surface. "Yes, and through there," he pointed toward an open door, "is the master bath. It has been updated with the addition of a shower and a new bath, both large enough for two."

The image of her and Ash sharing the shower, her and Ash reclining in the tub, her and Ash making love, filtered into her consciousness.

Why, oh, why, had she believed she could remain detached knowing how much she'd been drawn to him since that first time he'd kissed her? She had to remain emotionally detached even while occupying the same house, the same bed. Or the same tub.

"That sounds nice," Karen said. "What do you plan to do about furnishing this room?"

"That would be up to you. I have arranged for an open

account at the best furniture store in the city. You may choose anything you like.''

''Don't you want to have some say in it?''

''I trust your judgment, as long as the bed is comfortable and accommodating.''

Beds, Karen thought. More than one bed. More than one bedroom. Ash could have this one. He deserved to have this one. After all, he had paid for the house. She could take one of the others, stay there in her own bed. A lovely, lonely bed instead of sharing one with Ash. Yes, that would be best. That would be totally unappealing, but necessary if she wanted to remain emotionally grounded. She would have to broach that subject carefully so as not to anger him more.

Karen walked to the paned, double doors that opened to a wood plank porch surrounded by a low brick wall covered in clinging vines. The land sloped toward the harbor where various craft moved across the water. She could only imagine what a scene the panorama would present at sunrise and sundown. ''This is very nice.''

''The wall allows for some privacy if you are seated.''

Karen suddenly realized Ash was standing behind her, very close considering his cologne and deep voice wafted around her like a fine, sensual mist. ''Then I guess we could add a patio table, maybe some lounge chairs and have our morning coffee there without having to get dressed.''

''I suppose that people could do whatever they wish there without getting dressed.'' Ash's voice was low, deep, boldly seductive.

The words seemed to hang in the air along with a sudden spark of electric tension.

''You said the rest of the bedrooms are upstairs?'' Karen asked, annoyed by the tremor in her voice.

"Yes. This suite was added on at some point in time. It is totally segregated from the other living quarters. There is a small room across the corridor that would serve as a temporary nursery until our child is older."

"That's a good thing." Ash's close proximity was not, Karen decided. Ash's hands on her shoulders were not. Her reaction to his touch was not.

It took every ounce of Karen's fortitude to keep from turning around, turning into his arms and turning up the heat. Although right now, she felt as if she were about to go up in a blaze of glory despite the coolness of the room.

Before Karen could give everything over to a need for him that seemed determined to run a course she couldn't control, Ash dropped his hands and stepped away.

"Shall we see the upstairs now?" he asked.

Karen turned from the doors and met his dark gaze. She saw a glimpse of undeniable desire. The same desire she imagined was reflected in her own eyes.

"Yes, let's go upstairs," she said, sounding too harried, too uncomfortable. "I'd like to see the layout of the bedrooms. I'm sure I could find one that suits my needs."

"Does this one not suit your needs?"

"Oh, it's wonderful, but I think it should be yours."

"I would prefer we share this one."

Karen detected another hint of anger in his tone. "I'm not sure that's a good idea."

He reached out and traced a fingertip down the line of her jaw. She noticed a softness in his eyes she had never seen before. "I am only asking for a chance for us to get to know each other better, Karen. That is most important to me. That and making certain that you have all that you need while you're carrying our child. I ask that you please allow me that much. As per the terms of our arrangement, I will not touch you unless you ask it of me.''

Karen supposed she could allow him to share her bed temporarily, as long as he still agreed to forgo any real intimacy once she was pregnant. She couldn't allow him to take control of her life...or her heart. But as he continued to regard her with his dark, assessing eyes, one thing became all too clear.

Living with Ash might prove to be incredibly difficult—because falling for him could be all too easy.

The drive back into the city was spent in silence. Ash was still reeling from Karen's concern about what would become of the house if they parted ways. His concern centered on what would become of him. He refused to be shoved out of her life and their child's life should she attempt to discard him like yesterday's market report.

He would simply have to try harder to convince her that they should remain together. How he would do that, he had no idea. Or perhaps he did. One thing existed between them that could not be denied—desire. Fortunately that was one aspect he could use to his advantage. That and quite possibly his temporary absence from her life.

While Karen had been upstairs surveying the rooms, Ash had received a call from an overseas investor requesting his services. Though Ash would have preferred not to leave, he had been forced to agree to a planning meeting in Europe or lose the lucrative deal. On a positive note, distance might aid him in his cause with his reluctant wife. And he was probably a fool to think that Karen might miss his company.

When they pulled up at the curb several feet from Baronessa, he put up the convertible's top to allow more privacy and shifted in the seat to face Karen. "I need to speak to you about tonight," he said. "I'm afraid that I have been called away on business. I must leave immediately."

She looked somewhat displeased. "Today?"

"This evening."

"Then we won't be able to..." She flailed her hands about for a moment before clasping them in her lap. "You know."

"Make love? I am afraid not. This cannot wait."

"Neither can I. I mean...I only have a couple of fertile days left."

"If we have not yet achieved conception, our attempts will have to be postponed until next month." And he would be insane between now and that time if he could not touch her.

"You'll be gone a month?" The disappointment in her tone pleased Ash.

"I foresee no more than two weeks."

More silence ensued until she finally said, "What time does your plane leave?"

"At 6:00 p.m."

"I won't be off work until seven."

Ash reached across the console and patted her stocking-covered thigh, letting his hand linger there. "I suppose duty calls."

"Yes, I guess you're right."

She toyed with the top button of her blouse and the simple gesture made Ash's blood boil, his body come to life. He wanted her now. He wanted her to want him. Perhaps he could convince her to take the afternoon off, to take the opportunity to spend their last moments together engaged in some pleasurable activities. However, he would not try to convince her with words.

He drew a slow path from her knee to immediately beneath the hem of her skirt, wishing he had bought a sedan with a bench seat to give him better access. "It seems we are at cross-purposes due to our responsibilities."

She kept her eyes fixed on the dashboard. "Yes, we are."

He drew circles on her thigh with a slow fingertip. "It is a shame, not having the time or opportunity to spend our evening together."

"Yes. A real shame."

"Of course, I suppose we could consider returning to the hotel for an hour or so, but then I do have to pack."

"And I really need to get back to work."

He inched his hand higher. "Are you certain?"

She still refused to look at him. "No… Yes. I'm sure Mimi's wondering where I am."

With his free hand, he cupped her jaw and drew her face around to give her a kiss. She responded with an ardor that matched his own, with the soft play of her tongue against his leaving no doubt in Ash's mind that she wanted him, too.

After breaking the kiss, he said, "Come to the hotel with me."

Ash saw a trace of indecision in her eyes then a determined look that he did not care for. "I have to go to work now, and you have to get ready for your trip."

He stroked his thumb along the inside of her thigh. "Are you certain you would not like more memories to keep while I'm away? We would not have to return to the hotel."

Her shallow breathing told Ash she most certainly

might. "In a car in broad daylight, where anyone could see us?"

"Would anyone blame me for bringing my wife pleasure?"

She closed her legs tightly, trapping his hand, halting his upward progress. "We can't do it here. We'll be arrested. Besides, there's not enough room."

He bent his lips to her ear and whispered, "There are many ways to make love, Karen, regardless of the location. I am willing to show you."

She pulled his hand away and placed it in his lap. "I think we both need to remember the terms. We don't make love after I'm pregnant. Otherwise, it will only complicate things."

"Then we will not make love unless you make the request." Determination to break down her resistance, as she had so easily broken his, hurtled through Ash on the heels of his anger and his insatiable need for this woman. "And you will ask me, Karen. You most definitely will."

Karen hadn't asked Ash to make love to her. Of course, he'd been out of town for fifteen days, ten hours and twenty minutes, give or take a few. Even though she'd occupied her time with her work at Baronessa and supervising the house's remodeling, she still thought of him throughout the day and well into the night. Thought often of his kisses, his touch, his lovemaking—when she wasn't considering what to do about the sleeping arrangements when he returned.

As of two days ago, she had vacated the apartment after moving the few belongings she'd brought from Montana into the house. The workers had put the finishing touches on the master suite—an elegant rose-patterned paper on one wall of the bedroom, new Italian tile in the bath, newly restored hardwood floors—before starting renovations on the kitchen. The first go-round of furniture had been delivered yesterday, including the king-size four-poster bed, the only bed she had ordered so far. And just thinking about occupying it tonight, alone, magnified Karen's loneliness, a loneliness that had haunted her since Ash's departure. The same loneliness she had intimately known before she'd come to Boston.

Several times she had talked with Maria, thankful that her cousin sounded much less heavy-hearted, but even those conversations hadn't filled the empty space in Karen's soul. Neither had Ash's occasional calls, most made while she was at Baronessa. He hadn't said anything out of the ordinary, only basic inquiries about the house and her job, yet Karen was more aware of what he hadn't said—that he missed her.

All for the best, Karen told herself repeatedly. She already had too many confusing emotions running around in her head. She would be better off keeping the relationship with Ash on a platonic level—unless she wasn't pregnant. And in a matter of moments, she would find out.

Karen was only three days late but the test guaranteed that was enough time to see the results. While she readied for work, she made a point not to look at the white stick sitting on the jade-colored marble vanity before the allotted time had passed, even though the temptation was overwhelming.

Standing before the mirror, Karen braided her unruly hair as the seconds turned into minutes. She brushed her teeth, resisting another urge to sneak a peek. She applied her lipstick and sent a coral smudge down her chin at the sound of her watch's alarm, signaling the moment of truth had arrived.

After fumbling for the button to cut off the annoying shrill, Karen couldn't seem to force her feet to move. Funny, she had been so eager to end the suspense and now she was almost afraid—afraid of being disappointed. Maybe even a little afraid of the reality of bringing a child into the world with a man she found so very hard to resist. A man very in control of his world.

Karen swiped the lipstick smudge away from her chin with a tissue and only then did she approach the test. Her hand trembled as she reached out to take it, her pulse thrummed in her ears, her heart pummeled her chest.

She lifted the stick and studied the results for a split second, looked away, looked back, then looked away again. The answer to her question, to her dreams, finally registered.

Positive.

She was pregnant. Pregnant and stunned, happy and scared, crying in celebration of the miracle. And in the silence of the bathroom, in a deserted house, she had no one with whom to share the news. Not even the man who had made this possible, the father of her baby.

Karen supposed she could call Ash although she wasn't sure about his schedule, and she also wasn't sure this kind of news should be delivered by phone. He had told her he might be coming back to Boston tomorrow, but then he had told her he would only be gone for two weeks.

Maybe she should have waited until his return to take the test, but somehow Karen hadn't really expected it to be positive. Besides, the sooner she learned the results, the better. Now she could begin to prepare, make appointments, change her eating habits, lay off the caffeine. Now she could rest assured that her goal had been met, the conception completed and she had no reason to make love with Ash.

She might not have a reason, but that didn't make her want him any less.

Karen moved through her day at Baronessa in a euphoric haze, smiling often yet experiencing a bout of wistfulness when she waited on one family with two charming little girls. Her heart felt heavy as she witnessed the love and affection in the doting parents' expressions as they looked at each other, looked on patiently as the girls' exuberance came out in boisterous behavior over an outing that involved ice cream.

She found herself imagining what it would be like to have that closeness in her life, to have a man whose love for her was obvious even to an ordinary bystander. To have a child look at her with a different yet no less important love.

At least she would have her baby. At least she wouldn't be completely alone.

By the time Karen returned to the house that evening, her feet ached, her mind swam and she couldn't seem to shake the subtle yearning. After having a light supper in the form of a heart-healthy TV dinner, she took to the shower and stayed until the water turned cold, touching her belly every now and then as if that might make it real. But it still wasn't real to her. Maybe when she told Ash the news it might sink in. If she ever saw him again.

On her way out of the bathroom, Karen checked the test again, irrationally believing that the results had changed, only to find they remained the same. She was still pregnant, thrilled to be pregnant, and still lonely.

Karen retrieved her gown from the end of the bed but hesitated before slipping it on. Instead, she studied the two closets across the room, both seeming to sum up her relationship with Ash. Two people cohabitating in the same bedroom, two people from two different worlds practically living two separate lives.

She opened the door to the closet containing Ash's clothing that he'd had moved to the house after he took ownership. Several times she had surveyed his belongings but she'd never touched a thing. Tonight she gave into an urge she didn't understand and ran a hand along the row of suits and shirts. She came upon one hanger that held a long white linen robe with metallic gold trim interspersed with burgundy. An official-looking Arabian robe. She'd never seen him wear it, yet she could imagine it on Ash, imagine him looking regal and stately and incredibly handsome.

Like some lonely wife dressing in her absent husband's oxford shirt, Karen took the robe from its hanger, dropped the towel secured around her and slipped it on over her naked body. The fabric felt somewhat scratchy against her skin and it was much too long in the sleeve and hem. Still, she had no desire to remove the garment or to take away the lingering scent that was so unique to Ash. Wearing it made her feel closer to him somehow even though miles separated them, both physically and emotionally.

"Do you find my *djellabah* satisfactory?"

Caught. It was Karen's only thought when she heard the compelling voice coming from behind her.

She was still caught—caught between wanting to slink underneath the hanging clothes to hide out with the shoes, and needing to make sure she wasn't dreaming.

She chose the latter and turned to find Ash standing in the open bedroom door, looking dark and intense and beautiful. But he wasn't smiling. In fact, he looked almost angry. Then she noticed a box in his hand—the packaging for the pregnancy test she had so carelessly discarded atop the vanity instead of in the trash where it belonged.

Her gaze zipped from the box to his intense eyes full of questions. "I didn't know you'd come in."

"I am most definitely here and have been since early this afternoon."

"Where were you?"

"On the second floor in a room that I have set up as an office. The equipment was delivered today while you were at work."

She had prepared her dinner and taken a shower totally clueless. And he hadn't even bothered to make his presence known. "Did you not hear me come in?"

"I was aware of your arrival."

"And you didn't tell me?"

He raised the all but forgotten box. "Is there something you perhaps would like to tell me?"

Karen hugged her arms around her waist, suddenly chilled. "The rabbit kicked the bucket."

"The rabbit?"

She couldn't suppress her joy that came out in a smile. "I'm pregnant."

Karen waited for his reaction, waited for a grin, for a hug, for him to speak. He only stood there, silent and sullen.

"Aren't you going to say something?" Karen asked, unable to wait any longer to know what he was thinking.

"I'm pleased."

Pleased? He was simply pleased? Her smile disappeared. "Great. I'm thrilled. In fact, this is the most wonderful day of my life." Until he showed up with his lukewarm response to a life-altering occurrence.

For a moment he looked as though he might step forward, maybe even to hold her, something she desperately wanted at that moment. Instead, he said, "I have some business to attend to. I'll be upstairs."

He turned and walked away, leaving Karen alone wearing his robe and feeling as if she had just been dealt a severe blow to her heart. She told herself that his apathy was probably due to shock. Or maybe he was even a little afraid, same as her.

But Karen seriously doubted that anything would ever frighten Sheikh Ashraf ibn-Saalem.

Seven

Ash could not comprehend the fear that had almost consumed him over learning of Karen's pregnancy. He should be holding his wife, celebrating the impending birth of his child but instead he had escaped to the confines of his office.

Years ago he had learned that at certain times, detachment was required to remain focused. Tonight he could not begin to concentrate on work. He could only see Karen, the joy in her face when she'd announced the pregnancy. He could only consider how he had wanted to scoop her into his arms, kiss her into oblivion and take her to the bed in celebration.

Instead he had run from the worry that now that they had created a child, she might leave him much sooner despite the terms of their agreement. He had once been deserted by a woman whom he had loved with every thread of his being, only to face the sting of her betrayal when she had taken the money his own father had offered and left him without a glance.

Though he had survived, he had vowed to avoid repeating that mistake, pledged not to give in to those detrimental emotions, and for years he'd been successful. Until Karen.

What was it about her that had him doubting himself as a man? Regardless, he must consider his new wife. He must somehow convince her that what they had found together could lead to a solid future, if not a relationship formed by love. In order to do that, she deserved his utmost care and attention.

Ash shut down the computer and tossed aside the file folder to go in search of his bride. He found her in the master bedroom sitting on the edge of the mattress, a modest cotton nightgown covering her from neck to knees, a weathered and faded black book in her lap.

When she gazed up at him, Ash immediately noticed the tears. A strong surge of remorse, of protectiveness sent him forward, sent him to her side to wrap his arm around her delicate shoulder. "I am very sorry, Karen. You have obviously suffered from my disregard."

She swiped at her face with trembling fingers. "It's not only your reaction to the baby." She nodded toward the book. "It's this. My grandmother's journal. I was reading the part where she talks about bringing my father home after she stole him from the hospital, how she knew it was wrong."

Ash had heard the story from Daniel, had been told about the deaths of Karen's parents the year before, yet it had had little impact on him until now. "And she chose to keep a child that was not rightfully hers."

"Yes, but obviously she had a lot of guilt over that choice. That doesn't make it right, but I've forgiven her for it. I only wish I could have told her so before she died.''

He brushed a lock of her hair away from her cheek, now dampened with tears. ''You loved her greatly.''

''With all of my heart.''

''Ílli faat maat,'' he said.

''What does that mean?''

''The past is dead. Let bygones be bygones.'' Such sage words coming from someone who had been unable to follow his own advice. He had never forgiven his father. Most likely he never would.

Karen drew in a ragged breath then released it slowly. ''I had two wonderful grandparents and I couldn't have asked for a better mother or father. Now they're all gone and I can't even tell them about the baby.''

Ash held her tighter, experiencing more regret over how he had treated her earlier. ''I am here for you, Karen. I will be here for you and our child.''

She gave him a pleading look. ''Could you hold me for a little while?''

''I would most gladly do that.''

When Karen tossed back the covers and beckoned him into the bed, Ash realized that he would soon undergo a definitive test of strength. He removed only his shirt and shoes, believing that to be the best in this circumstance. They settled into the bed, her back to his chest with his arms securely around her. He fought his body's demands, the urge to strip out of his slacks and briefs, the need to cup her breasts in his palms, to peel the gown from her body and set a course over her naked flesh with his hands and mouth. Yet he recognized that she needed only solace.

Her breathing soon sounded steady and her body relaxed against his. His desire was still present, and so were the emotions threatening to surface from a place he had successfully kept shielded for many, many years.

Assured she now slept, Ash lowered his hand to Karen's soft belly that held their unborn child. She had given him the promise of new life and the hope that his legacy would live on. She had given him more than he'd ever thought possible.

His resistance waned as the emotional armor began to dissolve and in that moment, Sheikh Ashraf ibn-Saalem who had strove to be bound to no one, indebted to no one, was in grave danger of giving his new wife a liberal share of his heart, only to risk that she, too, would leave him.

In order to prevent history from repeating itself, he would not pressure her for intimacy. He would provide only comfort for however long it took to convince her to trust him. He would have to be content knowing that she needed at least that much from him now. Perhaps one day she would need more.

Karen couldn't believe how good she had felt over the past week. Her energy level was better than she'd ever imagined it to be considering her doctor had told her that morning that she might feel sleepy at times. Truth be known, she'd had trouble sleeping even though she had spent her nights in the security of Ash's arms since his return, engaged in quiet conversation and nothing more.

She'd had the devil of a time convincing him to wear some kind of clothes to bed because he preferred to sleep in nothing at all, but he'd finally agreed to pajama bottoms although he'd refused to wear a shirt. And oddly enough, he'd seemed happy to only hold her. Many times she had almost given in to the urge to turn to him and ask him to make love to her, but she hadn't. In part her pride had prevented her from doing so, but her concerns over becoming too emotionally tied to him had kept her from acting on the impulse. Whatever the reasons, she had avoided any intimate contact, and she was frankly going nuts. Maybe she would be a total fool to invite his complete attention, to ask him to make love to her, but she was beginning not to care about the darned arrangement or the original terms. Especially tonight.

While she had been finishing up the dinner dishes, he'd joined her in the not-quite-renovated kitchen immediately following his shower, something that had become a part of their routine. But even with him dressed in a plain white T-shirt and a pair of equally plain pajama bottoms, her covered in a short navy silk robe and intentionally nothing else, the process seemed anything but routine.

Every innocent contact they'd made while completing the task had Karen's lively libido coming to attention. Every whiff of his shower-fresh scent made her want to climb all over him without reservation. Every word he uttered, be it about his work or hers, sounded like bedroom talk to her ears.

"How have you been feeling?" he asked as he dried the last remaining pan.

Like a wicked, wanton female. "I'm feeling really good. I did have a craving today."

He smiled. "And what would that be?"

"Don't laugh."

"I will try to refrain."

"Olives. Spanish olives. I was in the middle of the dining room at work and I wanted one. Actually, I wanted the whole jar."

Ash released a slight chuckle. "I would have to say that is an odd craving."

If he only knew what else she'd been craving, he might

not be so surprised by the olives. Karen wagged a suds-covered finger at him. ''You said you wouldn't laugh.''

''My apologies. I'm pleased to hear you've been well.'' His expression turned suddenly serious. ''I am concerned that you are doing too much with your work at the gelateria and the renovations here.''

She shrugged. ''So far I have enough energy to handle it, so you don't have to worry.''

''The new appliances should be arriving by the end of the week. At least this dishwashing will not be necessary. I also believe I should begin interviewing housekeepers.''

Karen wanted to tell him that this activity wasn't so bad at all, especially since it provided the opportunity to spend more quality time with him at night, to know him better. She felt somewhat successful in that regard although he still retained a hint of mystery, enough to keep her guessing more often than not.

''I don't mind doing a few dishes,'' she said. ''Besides, it's only the two of us. We really don't need a housekeeper.''

''This is a large house, Karen. When the baby arrives, you'll not have much time to allow for upkeep.''

She slipped the final dish into the drainer. ''If you really think that's necessary, I suppose I wouldn't mind some help around here.''

''I will begin the interview process as soon as possible.''

She rested her damp hands on the edge of the sink. ''I think I should be involved, too. I don't want just anybody coming into the house.''

He raised a dark brow. ''Do you not trust my judgment?''

''I'm not saying that. I'd just like to be a part of the

process.'' She grinned. ''Besides, what if I want to hire a houseboy?''

Ash looked as if he'd just swallowed something bitter. ''You would wish to have a man tending to the chores?''

''Sure. Why not? I mean, you're drying the dishes, aren't you? And you're handling it quite well, I might add.''

The sensual look he now gave her was downright deadly. ''I enjoy working with my hands, although I have never used them on dishes before now.''

Karen was more interested in having him use his hands on her. As if he'd read her mind, he tossed the dish towel aside, reached around her to put away the plate in a cabinet while bracing a palm on her hip and pressing his body into her back.

Karen bit her lip to keep from blurting out, I want you here and now, on the drop cloths covering the floor, on the island bar, up against the refrigerator, anything to keep the hormones happy. After all, that was exactly what this uncanny, uncontrollable desire for Ash's attention was all about. A raging case of pregnancy hormones. At least that sounded logical.

Ash closed the cabinet door above Karen's head while she pulled the stopper from the sink. She froze with her hands in the disappearing water when his palms came to rest on her shoulders. ''Exactly what services would you require of a houseboy?'' His tone held a touch of amusement.

She sent him a teasing grin over one shoulder. ''You know, mopping the floors, vacuuming and, of course, the occasional massage.''

He lightly kneaded the muscles at her nape. ''Do you not like my massages?''

She tipped her head forward to give him better access. "Oh, you do all right in that department."

"Only all right?"

"Okay, better than all right. Especially when you hit the right spot." As far as Karen was concerned, he wasn't anywhere near that spot. Not yet, but he would be if she had any say in the matter.

Ash moved his massage to her lower back. "Is this better?"

Without thought of the consequences, Karen pulled his hand around to her breast and leaned back against him. All that solid, strong, warm maleness effectively incited her cravings—the ones not involving food—as well as her determination to have what she knew he could give her. "I could use a little attention here."

He palmed her breasts, rubbing his thumbs across her nipples, effectively bringing every inch of her to attention. "Is this satisfactory?"

Oh, yes. "You're getting there."

"Where is it you wish me to be?" His warm breath fanned her neck, fueled the fire.

She guided his palm from her breast to immediately beneath her belly. "I need..."

"What is it you need, Karen?" His coarse whisper made her shiver, made her want.

She reached back and slid her fingertips through his damp hair. "I need you, Ash. I need to be with you in every way."

"What are you asking of me?"

He knew exactly what she was asking, but if he wanted to hear her say it, Karen could definitely do that. "I'm asking you to make love to me."

"Are you absolutely certain?"

"Yes."

He pulled her hair away from her shoulder and planted soft kisses along her neck. ''Then perhaps we should retire to our bed.''

The bed seemed somehow too intimate. If they made love here in the kitchen, Karen could convince herself it was only sex, not lovemaking. She could trick her head into thinking that she was driven only by basic, biological urges. Convincing her heart was another matter altogether.

She pressed against Ash, finding him already aroused. No real surprise there. ''Forget about the bed. I don't want to wait.''

''I would not want to harm you or our child.''

She looked back at him. ''My doctor said that making love is fine.''

''You have seen a doctor?''

''Actually, this morning.''

He clasped her shoulders, turned her around and studied her with fierce, dark eyes. ''And you did not consider that I might wish to accompany you?''

Nothing like destroying the mood. ''They had a last-minute cancellation so there really wasn't time to call you. I had to take it or wait another month. Besides, I knew you were busy and it was only the first of many.''

He dropped his hands from her shoulders. ''Exactly. It was the first. I should have been there. I would have made the time.''

Karen had done everything for herself for so long, it hadn't occurred to her that something as simple as a doctor's appointment would mean so much to him. ''Today was only a routine exam. Everything's fine. You can come with me next month. They might do a sonogram then and we'll have our first picture.''

Ash strode from the kitchen and into the adjacent parlor without another word. Karen hurried to catch up to him, frustrated that he always seemed so determined to run away. She was determined not to let him this time. "Where are you going?"

"I am in need of some fresh air," he replied without slowing.

Once inside the bedroom, Ash threw open the French doors and walked onto the porch, stopping at the brick wall to stare at the harbor.

Karen came to his side while he stood white-knuckling the ledge as if he wanted to tear it apart with his bare hands. "So that's it, huh? I asked you to make love to me exactly as you said I would and now you're no longer interested?"

"Perhaps I'm not in the mood."

She let out a humorless laugh. "That's not what your mood indicator was telling me in the kitchen."

He kept his profile to her but she could still see his anger in the hard set of his jaw. "I cannot deny that I want you, but I also cannot deny that I am disappointed that you did not think to involve me today."

"I'm sorry, Ash." And she sincerely was. "I don't know what else I can say."

He sent her a brief glance before returning his attention to the glistening sea stretched out before them. "I would ask for your promise that you will consider me from this point forward when it comes to our child."

In any other instance, Karen might have argued he was being unreasonable. But right now she didn't want this night to end in bitter words and wounded feelings. She wanted to end it in his arms—a place where she could lose herself in a passion that defied common sense. "I promise. It won't happen again."

"Good."

Karen swallowed her pride and found it much easier going down than she'd expected. ''Since that's settled, do you think maybe we could take up where we left off in the kitchen?''

Ash remained silent for a moment then pushed away from the wall. Karen's heart dropped to her bare feet when she assumed he was about to go back inside. Instead he came up behind her and folded his arms around her middle, pulling her back against him. ''A remarkable view, do you not agree?''

Karen didn't care about the view. She didn't care about anything at the moment aside from making love with him. Although she felt secure and safe in his strong arms, she wanted more than security. She needed more than to be held. She was afraid to ask him again, afraid of his rejection.

She rested her arms loosely over his. ''Yes, it's a nice view. Whoever built the house did a remarkable job with the layout.''

''I've been told that the original owner was a sea captain,'' he said. ''He was gone for months at a time while his wife waited for his return. I imagine she probably stood in this very spot, watching for his ship's arrival.''

''A very romantic notion.'' Provided they cared about each other, Karen thought. How nice to consider that someone's love story had unfolded in the place where she and Ash now stood—two people whose future together was no more than a huge question mark beyond the present.

Ash slipped one hand immediately beneath the opening of her robe at her collarbone, keeping his other arm at her waist. ''I can only imagine their reunion after spending such a lengthy time apart.''

Karen could only imagine Ash's hand on her breast

again, but she decided to proceed with caution and allow him to take the lead, at least for now. "I'm sure the reunion must have been passionate. If neither one of them took lovers while they were separated."

"He would not be in need of another lover." He lowered his palm in small, tantalizing increments, until it came to rest immediately above her breast. "His wife would be all that he needed, and she would not be in need of another man."

"Then he must have been one incredible lover."

Finally Ash cupped her bare breast beneath the robe, causing Karen's breath to hitch hard in her chest. He thumbed her nipple slowly, gently. "Pleasing his wife would be of the utmost importance."

The conviction in Ash's tone caused Karen to shiver. "Do you think they made love in our bedroom?"

He rimmed the shell of her ear with his clever tongue. "Perhaps they never made it beyond this porch. Perhaps he lifted her skirts and undid his trousers and took her right here because he could not wait."

Karen felt the tug of the sash at her waist as well as the strong pull of desire. "I could understand his hurry." At the moment she wanted Ash to hurry but as usual he took his time, grazing his warm lips across her neck as he slowly opened her robe, allowing the cool ocean air to breeze over Karen's bare skin. The wisp of wind did nothing to alleviate the heat jetting through her entire body.

"I suppose had they chosen to make love here," he continued, "someone might have seen them."

"Maybe that's why they built this wall." Karen's voice sounded coarse with need as visions of Ash making love to her on the porch flickered in her hazy brain.

He planted his palm above her belly while he continued to fondle her breast with the other. ''True, but the wall only offers so much privacy if one is standing. Any passing sailor would have seen what they were doing.''

''Only if he had some high-powered binoculars, and I'm not sure they made those back then,'' Karen said, proud that she had come up with a solid argument at such a mindless time.

''But they most certainly have those now.'' He circled a fingertip around her navel, sending Karen's heart into a mad dash against her chest. ''Perhaps someone is watching us.''

She again nudged her bottom against Ash, hoping to encourage him, finding he didn't need any encouragement. ''Are you saying we should continue this inside?''

''Only if you so desire.''

She only desired him, longed for what he could give her. Here. Now. ''Why should we? We're hidden enough. No sailor could tell what we're doing.''

Ash skated his fingertips through the covering of curls between her legs. ''He could most certainly tell.''

Karen drew in another sharp breath as he made one slow pass over her flesh, then another, not quite hitting the mark. ''How would he know?''

He began to ply her with gentle, breath-stealing strokes, this time directing his attention exactly where she needed it the most. ''Even if he could not see what I'm doing, he would recognize it by your expression alone.''

An almost guttural sound escaped Karen's lips as Ash worked his magic to appease the ache, as he continued to speak to her in a deep, hypnotic voice that caressed her as surely as his skilled hand. ''He would know how I am touching you. He would envy me.''

Ash effectively fed the firestorm in Karen with only a

few well-chosen words and well-placed caresses. When the wind picked up in intensity, so did Ash's stroking.

"Can you imagine what he is seeing in your face, Karen, knowing it's only moments before you give in?"

Karen closed her eyes, not yet wanting to let go of the pleasure. But she could do nothing, *nothing,* to stop it, when Ash whispered, "He would know, Karen. He would know the moment I made you—"

Karen rode surge after surge of a climax that hit her with a resounding fury. Her body trembled, her legs felt as if they might give way, but Ash was there, holding fast to her as she fought to recover her respiration. Ash brought her face back and dipped his head to kiss her, his tongue deftly advancing then withdrawing between her parted lips, reminding her that she still wanted more. She wanted it all.

She started to turn in his arms but he stopped her with a firm, "No," and an equally firm grasp on her shoulders.

He stepped back and Karen regarded him over one shoulder to find him twisting his shirt over his head. His beautiful, bare chest took on a copper glow as it reflected the last remnants of the sun. He snaked out of his pajama bottoms, revealing his complete arousal, and Karen was completely at his mercy.

He came back to her and nudged her legs apart with his palms. "Open for me, Karen."

She did as he asked without question yet she wasn't at all sure how this was going to work. He slipped her robe from her shoulders, bunched it between her and the wall and said, "Cross your arms on the ledge."

Again, she did as he asked and again she looked over her shoulder. "Ash, are you sure—"

"There are many ways to make love, Karen." She felt

the gentle nudge of his erection. "You only need to trust me."

Karen did trust him, trust that he would take good care of her, and she wasn't wrong to do so. He guided himself inside her then braced her hips with his palms, angling her away from the wall. Karen rested her forehead on her folded arms to absorb the sensations as Ash curled into her, filling her body completely, his chest so solid against her back, one arm folded around her middle, one hand drifting lower to touch her again. With her senses heightened to the surroundings, she was mildly aware of the sound of lazy waves lapping against the shore in the distance, Ash whispering lyrical words she didn't understand yet whose meaning became quite clear as he rocked against her, setting a calm cadence at first, then moving faster, deeper. So close, she thought as she moved in sync with Ash. So close, as if they were remarkably one body, completely in tune with each other.

All sounds gave way to Ash saying her name over and over as he continued to move inside her. After one long, deep thrust, Karen gave in to another floor-tilting release and Ash went taut against her with his own.

After a time, he pulled away, moved in front of her, leaned back against the wall and took her into his arms. She relished the feel of their damp, bare skin touching at every point, relished the strong beat of his heart against her cheek, the way he leisurely slid his fingertips up and down her spine. The way he took all her weight, a solid cushion against the wall that couldn't be too comfortable on his own back. Yet he continued to hold her as if that didn't matter, as if her comfort was all that mattered. As if *she* was all that mattered.

The sky had turned a mix of muted grays and pinks, and a few stars appeared on the horizon along with a sprinkling of lights around the harbor. The air had grown considerably colder, but Karen didn't care. As far as she was concerned, they could stay like this all night.

When Ash tensed, Karen glanced up to find he looked troubled. "What's wrong?"

He smoothed a hand through her hair. "I was much too rough in light of your condition."

She kissed his chin and gave him a reassuring smile. "I guarantee I bear no bruises."

"I should have been more considerate," he said. "I should be more careful with you."

"Ash, it's really okay. Junior is barely walnut-sized. When I get big and fat, then you might have to be more careful." She laughed from the joy of that thought. "Or maybe I'll have to be careful not to crush you."

Finally, he smiled. "Then I can assume we will enjoy more of these moments?"

How could she refuse? How could she give up what she'd found with him? She could take what he offered from a physical standpoint and simply remember to keep a firm grip on her emotions. At least she hoped she could. "If you're really, really good to me, I guess we can do this again. If not, I'm definitely hiring that houseboy. Or maybe even a sailor."

He lightly kissed her lips. "I plan to be very good to you. You will not require another man. But now you need to retire to bed."

Karen shrugged and grinned. "Fine by me. I have no objections to continuing this in the bedroom."

"You need to sleep."

Not that again. "I'm not at all sleepy. Besides, I need another bath with all this humidity, not to mention our recent activities."

His smile returned. ''Are you registering a complaint about our activities?''

''Not at all. I just feel a little sticky.''

He ran his hands along her bottom and tugged her fully against him. ''You feel quite good, in my opinion. But a bath will most certainly help you relax. I will draw one for you.''

Ash kissed her forehead, moved her aside then walked toward the bedroom with masculine grace, without hesitation, as always totally comfortable with his nudity. Karen, on the other hand, felt a little more inhibited now faced with the reality of the situation. She was standing naked on a deck at dusk. At least they didn't have any neighbors close by. Determined to remedy the situation, she grabbed her robe from where it had landed on the floor, slipped it on and bent to gather Ash's discarded clothes.

''Are you coming inside or do you wish to taunt the sailor some more?''

Karen straightened and saw Ash standing in the open doors to the bedroom, still naked, his arms folded across his broad chest. Another swift rush of heat spiraled through her, settling in intimate places that should be more than satisfied, but weren't, thanks to her husband standing there looking like some magazine centerfold.

She joined Ash inside the bedroom where she tossed his clothes onto the bed. ''Do you want to take a bath with me?''

He looked mock-surprised. ''What has become of my cautious wife?''

Gone from the premises. ''Maybe she just can't get enough of her husband.''

He stroked his whisker-shadowed jaw and grinned. ''Ah. That could prove to be very interesting.''

"I certainly hope so."

Karen took Ash's offered hand and followed him into the bathroom where he turned on the water in the tub. He removed her robe again, paused to kiss her again, before he helped her up the two steps and into the now-full bath. Instead of joining her, much to Karen's disappointment, he remained on the top step and told her, "I will see to your needs."

And he did, beginning with washing her hair, kneading her scalp with firm yet gentle strokes. He even managed to avoid getting too much water in her eyes while rinsing the shampoo away. After that, he squeezed a large dab of rose-scented shower gel in his palm and bathed her from forehead to toes, taking his time with his ministrations. Karen watched with growing interest and building desire as he lingered at her breasts then slipped his hand beneath the water to touch her again.

When Karen realized his intent, she said, "Ash, I've already… Twice, in fact."

"You will again."

"But I'm not sure I can again." She wasn't sure if she could take it if she could.

"Do not underestimate yourself, Karen." He caressed her with tempered, tender strokes. "Do not underestimate me."

Who could argue that? It was Karen's last thought when Ash began another sensual assault with his talented hands. He was so thorough with his touch, so smooth with his moves, slipping a finger inside her just as another orgasm claimed her with as much force as the others.

After the shock waves subsided, Karen stared at Ash in awe. She'd had three climaxes tonight. Three. Obviously she'd been saving them up, or maybe it was simply

Ash's skill. Ash, who looked mighty proud at the moment.

''Did I not tell you it would happen again?'' he said.

His arrogance caused her to blurt out, ''How do you know I wasn't faking it?''

''I would greatly question a man who could not discern pretend from reality.''

Carl shoved his way into Karen's mind, not a welcome thought at all. ''Believe me, those men do exist.''

''In my opinion, that is total sacrilege, not knowing when you have pleased a woman or not.'' He bent his head and circled his tongue around one nipple, then the other.

Karen struggled to remain coherent. ''Maybe some women are better at pretending.''

He raised his head and frowned. ''Trust me, I would know whether you were pretending.''

Little did he know, she had been pretending—pretending that she didn't have feelings for him. And if she wasn't careful, Karen was afraid he would see right through that pretense. ''Exactly how much experience have you had with other women?'' Now why had she asked that at a time like this?

Ash nudged her legs farther apart with his palms, touched her again and darned if she wasn't excited again. ''Whatever has happened in my past, in your past, does not matter,'' he said. ''What happens between us does.''

Karen couldn't take his absence in the tub any longer. She splashed water in his face, bringing about Ash's luminous grin. ''You can either get in here with me now, or I'm getting out and we can initiate the new floor.''

He looked down at the tile beneath his feet. ''Far be it for me to argue since the floor would be less than comfortable.''

Ash slid into the tub where they faced each other. After sinking into the water, he lifted Karen's leg over his thigh then slipped inside her.

She absorbed the taste and feel of his tongue as he kissed her, welcomed the absolute power of his body as he moved in perfect step with hers. Somehow he found an erogenous zone she didn't know she owned and she shattered again. He whispered her name as he reached his climax with a shudder and a sharp breath.

Karen felt weak, thoroughly satisfied and unequivocally lost. She wondered how this could feel so right. She wondered how she could even consider giving her heart to a man who was everything she'd been determined to avoid. A man who clung to his control as steadfastly as the Boston ivy clung to the trellis outside the window. How could she ever learn to accept that aspect of him when she had battled for her own independence time and again with Carl?

Carl was an overbearing guy-type who refused to see women as anything but a necessary commodity. Ash had an inherent tenderness beneath the steely facade. A tenderness he'd shown her at times, especially during lovemaking. But could she ever trust that he wouldn't try to keep her under his thumb?

Karen didn't want to think about that right now. She only wanted to lie in her husband's arms, cherish these wondrous moments.

After a time, she finally said, "That was exactly what I needed."

"Let us not forget your need for olives," Ash said with an endearing chuckle followed by another tender kiss. "I will buy you olives. I will buy you cases of olives, if that is what you desire. Whatever you wish from me, you only need ask."

Would she be wrong to one day ask him to love her? Would she be crazy to fall in love with him?

Crazy or not, it was only a matter of time, if it wasn't already too late.

Eight

"Are you Luke Barone's child?"

Karen pivoted on the sidewalk in front of Baronessa's entrance to find a black-clad elderly woman with thinning white hair and deep-set brown eyes glaring at her. She stood next to a dark blue sedan parked at the curb where a driver leaned back against the hood. Had it not been for that, Karen might have assumed the woman to be homeless.

"Luke was my father. I'm Karen Saalem. Who are you?"

The woman took a tentative step toward Karen. "It doesn't matter who I am, but one thing you must know. As a member of the Barone family, you, too, will be cursed."

Karen felt as if she'd been set down in the middle of some voodoo B movie. She might have been more wary if the woman hadn't been so frail and looked so harmless, except for her severe eyes. ''Well, I don't really believe in curses so I guess I'll take my chances.''

''You should believe,'' the crone warned. ''You are no different from the rest. You'll be cursed to love a man who will never love you.''

Karen had heard about all of the melodrama she could take. Through a false smile she said, ''Have a nice day,'' then walked into the shop.

Daniel sat at the counter with a cup of coffee in hand, a smile to greet her. ''Hey, if it's not the sheikh's wife.''

Karen tossed her purse beneath the counter. ''Actually, today it appears I'm a Barone and cursed.''

Daniel inclined his head, looking confused. ''Care to explain that?''

She nodded toward the window where the woman still stood. ''Some strange lady stopped me outside and told me I'm cursed.''

Daniel slipped from the barstool and peered out the windows. ''What is she doing here?''

''I have no idea,'' Karen said. ''I don't even know who she is.''

Daniel reseated himself at the counter and took a long drink of coffee as if it were whiskey. ''She's Lucia Conti and she's nothing but trouble.''

Karen leaned on the counter. ''You mean *that* Lucia Conti? The one who despises the entire Barone clan? Maria mentioned her to me when I first came to Boston but I guess I didn't realize she was still around.''

''Yeah, she's still around. And she's been cursing the family since the thirties. The old Valentine's Day curse. Oddly enough, some strange things have happened on Valentine's Day, including your father's kidnapping.''

Karen was too pragmatic to believe in curses and more

inclined to believe in coincidences. ''Well, guess I'm officially a part of the family now.''

She made the remark with a touch of humor but Karen couldn't disregard Lucia's words. Was she in love with a man who couldn't love her in return? Ash had never said he loved her last night, but then she hadn't told him either. Besides, curses were for fools. Love could be too, if one wasn't loved in return.

She turned her attention back to Daniel. ''What are you doing here so early in the morning?''

''I have a couple of things I need to ask you.''

Karen tied her apron around her waist and shoved a pencil behind her ear. ''Shoot.''

''The whole family is wondering about Maria. Since you two are so close, and since you were the last person to see her, I decided to ask if you know where she is.''

Uh-oh. ''She's taking a vacation.''

Daniel appeared skeptical. ''Without telling anyone? I find that kind of weird.''

Karen wasn't sure how she should answer. She also wasn't sure why Daniel's voice had taken on a tinny quality, or why her vision had begun to blur and her limbs felt weighted. She was vaguely aware of Mimi standing behind her, of the door opening and someone coming inside, mildly cognizant of the fact that her legs felt like mush and in about two seconds they wouldn't be able to hold her as she began to wilt and fade like a week-old flower....

When Karen came to, she was on her back on the floor behind the counter, someone's coat propped under her neck. Daniel was crouched beside her and Mimi was hovering above her. ''Call nine-one-one,'' Daniel said. ''Then call her husband.''

Karen gathered her strength and raised her head. ''No!

I'm fine. It was just a dizzy spell. I haven't had any breakfast yet.''

Mimi knelt and with Daniel's assistance helped Karen up into a sitting position. Karen was thankful that today she'd opted to wear slacks. Otherwise, her skirt would probably be around her neck about now.

''Are you sure you're okay?'' Daniel asked with concern.

Karen still felt somewhat light-headed but much better than she had a few moments ago. ''I'm okay.'' She glanced at Mimi. ''Could you come with me into the restroom, Mimi? I need to splash some water on my face.''

''No problem, missy. If you're sure you can walk.''

''I won't know unless I try.''

Mimi and Daniel helped her to her feet and she braced one hand on the counter. Once she was assured that everything was moderately okay, she took a baby step.

''I still think I should call a doctor,'' Daniel said.

''I'll call him in a little while. I'm sure I'll be fine as soon as I get something to eat.''

With Mimi holding on to her arm and Daniel trailing behind them, Karen walked cautiously toward the restroom. At the door Daniel told her, ''I'll be right outside if you need me.''

''We'll be okay,'' Karen told him, hoping that were true. Should she faint again, Mimi was too small to catch her.

''Good thing I caught you,'' Mimi said as Karen stood over the sink, splashing water in her face.

She studied Mimi from the mirror's reflection. ''You caught me?''

''Yes, right before you landed on the floor. So when is the baby due?''

Karen's pallor turned pink. "How did you know?"

Mimi patted Karen's back. "The fainting was my first clue but I guess you could say you have that glow about you."

After staring in the mirror at her disheveled hair and colorless lips, Karen decided she looked anything but glowing. "The baby's due in late May."

Mimi grinned. "Wonderful news! You know, I would've given my Johnny's favorite bowling ball to have a baby." Her sigh was wistful. "But we had each other."

Karen wiped her face with a towel, turned from the sink and leaned back against it. "You must have really loved each other."

"Very much." Mimi's mellow expression melted into a frown. "You, missy, need to take some time off. You're working too hard."

"But Maria would—"

"Rather walk across a blistering sidewalk barefoot than see something happen to you or your baby."

So would Karen. "I'll shorten my hours."

"I imagine your man will have something to say about that once he finds out about your spell."

Karen had no doubt he would, which was why she didn't intend to tell him. He would only worry and most likely insist that she quit her job. She wouldn't do that unless she was in danger of compromising the pregnancy. She would simply stay off her feet as much as possible, take several breaks and eat regular meals. "I'd prefer you not tell him."

Mimi clicked her tongue and shook her head. "Starting out your married life with secrets isn't a good thing at all."

True, Karen thought, but she was already keeping a

secret. A big secret. He had yet to know that she felt far more for him than only mere affection, despite the fact she didn't want to. "I'll think about what you're saying. In the meantime, let's get back to work. Veronica is probably rattled having to take care of the morning customers all by herself."

"She was that way the minute she walked in the door." Mimi drew Karen into a brief hug, taking both of them by surprise. "You be careful today. If you even begin to look the least bit shaky, I'm going to call your husband myself."

Karen had no doubt she would. "It's a deal. First I need to make a call to my doctor."

Mimi and Daniel stayed immediately outside the break room while Karen made the call to the doctor's office. She spoke with a nurse who assured Karen that it was, in fact, normal to have dizzy spells during pregnancy. She also told Karen that she would have the physician call her when he returned to see his afternoon patients.

After she hung up, Karen reentered the dining room and, at Mimi's insistence, took a seat by Daniel at the counter with a glass of milk and a cherry-filled pastry. While she nibbled on the roll, Daniel continued to stare at her.

She gave him a determined look. "I'm not going to fall off this stool, if that's what you're worried about."

He gave her his infamous grin. "You look like hell, Karen."

"Gee, thanks."

"Is your new husband wearing you out?"

She thought about the night before, their lovemaking. He was wearing her down, wearing her resistance down with every kiss, every touch. "Ash is fine, but I hope you won't tell him about this little incident."

"Don't you think he has a right to know? After all, he is your husband."

Yes, he was her husband, in name only—and a born protector who valued his control. Telling him that she'd fainted would only unearth that side of him. Things were going so well between them, she didn't dare upset the applecart. "Look, Daniel, if you must know, I'm pregnant. That's probably why I got a little dizzy. It's normal. I've promised Mimi I would take it easy."

He forked a hand through his brown hair and grinned. "I'll be damned. Congratulations. I'm not at all surprised Ash got you pregnant so quickly. He's pretty fast at everything he does."

Except for lovemaking, Karen thought. In that case, he was slow and easy in most instances. Again she recalled the night before on the porch, in the tub, the way he had loved every last inch of her so thoroughly. If she didn't quit thinking about that, she might faint again.

Karen concentrated on shredding the pastry to avoid Daniel's continued scrutiny. "How's Phoebe?"

"Phoebe is great. In fact, that's the other reason why I'm here. She wants us to have dinner together before we leave town again."

"I thought you just got back."

"We did, but we want to travel some, see the world. Phoebe likes a little adventure and I'm just the man to give it to her. Every day and every night."

No wonder Daniel and Ash were such good friends. They were both class-A rogues. After tossing aside the remnants of her pastry, Karen stood. She already felt much stronger.

"I hate to end our little visit, Daniel, but I have work to do."

''Okay,'' Daniel said as he stood beside her. ''But promise me you'll take care of yourself, okay.''

''Okay.''

''And tell Ash about today. If you don't, I will.''

Karen's mouth fell open. ''You wouldn't dare.''

Daniel took his jacket from the adjacent stool and slipped it on. ''Yeah, I will. You're a Barone, and you're stubborn like the rest of us. You're also family and I don't want anything to happen to you because of an overabundance of pride. Ash deserves a healthy, happy wife and child.''

Karen recognized that there was a good deal of logic in her cousin's words, but she wasn't sure that informing Ash of today's events would help their situation. She also realized he deserved the truth. ''Okay, I'll tell him.''

''Great,'' Daniel said then headed out the door.

Karen decided that if she sugarcoated the situation, told Ash that she had been a little dizzy today, then she could get by without concerning him too much.

She would tell him tonight, when she returned home.

Ash waited in the den for Karen's return, nursing a quarter-full tumbler of scotch while attempting to maintain some semblance of calm. Considering what he had learned an hour before, it was all he could do not to down the entire bottle.

He had found out about Karen's troubles first through Daniel, who had extended a dinner invitation for the evening if ''Karen was feeling up to it.'' Daniel had said no more other than Ash needed to ask his wife about something that had happened that morning. When he'd attempted to call Karen at Baronessa, Mimi had not been so discreet when she informed Ash that Karen had fainted. The waitress's assurances that no other episodes had occurred during the day had done nothing to quell Ash's concerns or his anger over Karen not bothering to call him immediately. Had he not learned that his bride was on her way, he would have gone to Baronessa's and insisted that she allow him to drive her home.

Ash had struggled with his own guilt over the possible role he had played in Karen's illness. Last night he had thought of nothing but his own desire to make love to her. She could very well have paid the price for his careless disregard of her condition.

From this point forward, he would implement the greatest of care, treat her in the way she deserved to be treated, even if that meant keeping his hands to himself until he was certain that lovemaking would not compromise Karen's health or their child's. A difficult prospect considering how much it had meant to have her ask him to make love to her, how much it had meant to hold her the way he had wanted since the day they had married, how much he'd begun to treasure each moment in her presence.

He battled his own wariness over the vulnerability she had begun to uncover within him. She was everything he desired in a woman, and everything he had feared when it came to matters of the heart. Yet when he heard the front door open, it took all his strength not to go to her and take her in his arms. Instead he forced himself to remain seated and struggled to keep his resolve intact.

Karen walked into the room and he immediately noticed the lack of color in her cheeks. "Hi, there." Her voice was as fragile as her smile.

Ash decided to maintain his composure and allow her the benefit of an explanation. "How was your day?"

She tossed her purse and keys onto the end table and collapsed onto the sofa. "Hectic."

"Nothing momentous occurred?"

She pulled her legs beneath her and rolled her neck on her shoulders. "Just the usual."

Ash took a long drink, leaned forward with his elbows braced on his knees and grasped the tumbler between his palms, his grip threatening to shatter the glass. "Fainting is a part of your normal routine?"

Karen straightened, her eyes wide with comprehension. "Did Daniel tell you?"

"No, not precisely. He did voice his concern over your health as well as his congratulations. Mimi, however, was quite frank."

She waved a hand in dismissal. "It was nothing. Only a dizzy spell."

Ash maintained a death grip on the glass while holding on to a thin thread of control. "I do not consider it to be nothing. You're doing too much. You're keeping insane hours at Baronessa then coming home to oversee the renovations. Your lack of sleep is also affecting your health as well as our child's."

"I've been getting plenty of sleep, with the exception of..." Her gaze wavered and a tinge of pink washed over her face. "Last night was an exception."

Last night was still fresh on Ash's mind, again feeding his guilt. "I am well aware that my behavior last evening could have contributed to your problems this morning."

She sighed. "Come on, Ash. We didn't engage in heavy calisthenics."

"We were careless. I was careless."

"You were very careful."

"Not on the porch."

"I told you, I'm not fragile. I also told Mimi that I needed to stay off my feet as much as possible. I can run the register while she and the staff wait on customers."

''And I told Mimi that you might not be returning to work for some time.''

Karen bolted from the sofa. ''You had no right to make that decision.''

''What would you have me do? If you will not take care of yourself, then I most certainly will do it for you.''

She clenched her hands at her sides. ''I don't need a keeper.''

Ash set his glass aside, rose and looked into her eyes. ''Do you sincerely believe that your current schedule is benefiting our unborn child or you?''

She hesitated a moment before her anger appeared once more. ''I wouldn't do anything, *anything,* to hurt this baby. It means everything to me!''

''Then you must stop and consider what is best.'' Ash decided that moderation in tone would be to his benefit. ''You have much to do with the work on the house and the preparation for our child's arrival. Would it not be best to complete those tasks?''

''But Maria's gone and Mimi—''

''Assures me she can handle Baronessa. You can maintain communication by phone and supervise from here. I'm certain Maria would find that agreeable.''

Karen lowered her eyes and rubbed a hand across her forehead. ''I guess you're right. My doctor did mention that I might want to take it easy for a few days.'' Her gaze snapped back to his. ''But after the restoration on the house is complete, I'll decide then whether to return to work.''

''I respect your decision.''

''And furthermore...'' She frowned. ''What did you say?''

''I said I respect your decision regarding your work.

However, I do hope that we can openly discuss your options when the time comes.''

A fleeting look of surprise passed over Karen's expression. ''Sure. I'm open to discussion. As long as you realize I can be pretty darned stubborn.''

''As I can be at times.''

A hint of a smile curled the corners of her full lips. ''Now why doesn't that surprise me?''

Right then Ash wanted nothing more than to hold her, yet he doubted the wisdom in that, doubted he would be satisfied with only an innocent embrace. Considering Karen's current problems, he would be wise to temper his need for her, even if it meant he would have to eventually sleep on the sofa. ''Daniel has invited us to join him and his new wife for dinner, if you are feeling well enough to do so.''

She tipped up her chin in determination. ''I'm feeling fine, thank you. I do need to take a quick bath first.''

He was immediately thrust back to their shared bath, their shared bodies. ''We are to meet them in an hour so you have time.''

''Good.''

Ash felt his control faltering with every remembrance of the night before. Felt his body stir to life. ''Do you need any assistance, should you become dizzy again?''

''I haven't been dizzy since this morning.'' Her smile was now in full bloom. ''And if you *help* me with my bath, we'll never be ready in an hour.''

With that she walked away, leaving Ash alone with the realization that in all of his years, he had never met anyone quite like Karen—a self-assured woman whose determination matched his own, whose sensuality and inner beauty drew him beyond desire. And in all of his years of learning, he had never been taught candid expression of his emotions. Yet there had been a time when he had given his all, bared his soul and left his heart open.

Perhaps it was time to face his fears and risk learning to feel again, for both his sake and his wife's. But if he chose that path, how would he deal with Karen's departure after their child's birth? If luck prevailed, he would never have to face that. He would simply have to try harder to convince Karen to stay, even if that meant opening old wounds.

Karen was determined to have a good time, not an easy feat when she watched Daniel and Phoebe from across the dinner table, watched the way Daniel softly stroked Phoebe's shoulder, occasionally touching her blond hair and hanging on her every word. Despite her jaded perspective, Karen found herself longing to have the same relationship, that same obvious, unconditional love. If only she could believe that that might happen with her husband.

At the moment she felt less than optimistic. Ash had his arm resting casually over her chair, but he'd failed to touch her. He'd barely spoken to her other than to ask her what she wished for dinner. At least he hadn't ordered for her, allowing her that much freedom. He hadn't scolded her, either, when she'd picked at her salmon and relinquished her plate to the waiter before finishing half the meal.

Logically, she understood Ash's concerns and she agreed that taking some time off would be good for her and the baby. But logic didn't come into play when her fears of being stripped of making her own decisions haunted her, or the fact that she was bordering on a love for him that seemed so completely unwise.

She regretted that she wanted him in her bed, wanted

him in her life despite the lack of wisdom in those wishes. Maybe the time would come when she'd be ready to make a commitment. And maybe he would tell her that she was wrong to expect more from him than his role as the father of her child. Was she willing to take that risk?

"Do you know about our cousin, Reese?"

Daniel's query interrupted Karen's musings, drawing her back into the conversation. She searched what remained of her brain. "Maria's brother?"

"Yeah," Daniel said. "One of Uncle Carlo's sons."

"I remember Maria mentioning him once. She said he's been gone for years."

"We saw him in Harwichport when we were on our honeymoon," Phoebe said. "No one in the family has seen him for a long time."

Daniel took a drink of wine. "You'd probably like him, Ash. He's used his trust fund to make a fortune as a day trader. Now he basically sails around the world in his schooner. I was surprised to see him back in the States."

"Considering the number of Barone cousins, I'm surprised I remembered his name," Karen said.

Phoebe laughed softly. "It's a large family. But the good thing is, you'll never be lacking in support."

Karen appreciated the support she'd received from both Daniel and Maria, yet at times she still felt alone. Or she had until Ash entered her life. "Why did Reese leave?"

"There was a scandal involving a woman," Daniel said. "A society deb who pinned her pregnancy on him. He refused to marry her even when Uncle Carlo and Aunt Moira insisted he do the right thing. As it turned out, the baby wasn't his after all. After that, he left and he hasn't been back. I think he felt somewhat betrayed by his parents' mistrust."

"I can certainly understand how that might drive a son from his parents' home," Ash said.

Karen was more than curious about the conviction mixed with anger in Ash's tone, but before she could ask him to elaborate, Daniel said, "Enough about the family. Let's toast the soon-to-be new addition."

Phoebe and Daniel raised their glasses of wine while Ash and Karen hoisted their water goblets. Ash had turned down any alcoholic beverages in deference to her condition, something Karen very much appreciated.

When they touched their glasses together, Daniel said, "To Ash and Karen and their baby to be."

"I was thrilled when Daniel told me you're pregnant, Karen," Phoebe said.

Ash touched Karen's face with a reverence she'd never before experienced. "And I am happy my wife has honored me with a child."

"To new life," Phoebe said then gave her smile to Daniel. "And to love."

Overcome with emotion, Karen was unable to hold back the threat of tears. She excused herself from the table and said, "I'll be back in a minute. I need to freshen up."

Ash caught her hand and studied her with concern. "Are you not feeling well?"

"I'm okay. Really." But she wasn't.

Karen rushed away from the table, ran from all the love radiating from Daniel and Phoebe. And in many ways she was very much trying to escape her feelings for Sheikh Ashraf ibn-Saalem, but she feared she was already now, and forever, his captive.

Nine

After they arrived home, Karen went immediately into the bathroom to prepare for bed. Many times during the return drive, she'd sensed Ash had wanted to say something, yet he'd remained silent, almost brooding. She had no idea what had brought about his melancholy mood. She had no doubt what had provoked hers. Confusion, plain and simple. So much she needed to ask him, so many things she should tell him.

When she left the bathroom, she found Ash standing on the opposite side of the bed wearing only his pajama bottoms as well as a guarded expression. As Karen began to turn down the covers, he asked, ''Would you prefer I sleep on the sofa?''

She paused with her hand on the sheet and stared at him. ''Why would I want that?''

''I thought you might be more comfortable having the bed to yourself.''

"It's a king-size bed, Ash. I barely know you're there." An out-and-out lie. She always knew when he was there, and when he wasn't.

"If you are certain."

She slipped beneath the sheet and patted the space next to her. "I'm sure."

After Ash settled in, Karen snapped off the light. The room went completely dark except for the muted light filtering in from the sheers covering the French doors. As he always did, Ash settled her against him with her back to his front, his arms wrapped securely around her. Silence pervaded and so did the questions whirling around in Karen's mind.

"Ash, are you awake?"

"Yes."

"Why do you think that two people as different as Phoebe and Daniel fall in love?"

"I suppose for some it's not a choice."

"Have you ever been in love?" When he didn't immediately answer, Karen added, "I'm sorry. It's really none of my bus—"

"Once."

The word echoed in the darkened bedroom. "Oh" was all Karen could think to say. She didn't want to push him but at least she now had hope that he was capable of loving someone.

"I was very young, and very foolish," he continued, surprisingly without Karen's prodding. "She was considered a commoner and my father disapproved. I had been willing to give up my title and inheritance for her, but instead she took the money that my father offered and walked away."

Karen could tell by his tone that the admission was costing him. "I'm sure that hurt quite a bit."

"I survived," he said. "I left my father's business immediately after that. We haven't spoken since."

"And how long ago was that?"

"Fifteen years."

Fifteen years? "What about your mother?"

"She died when I was in my teens."

It suddenly dawned on Karen that Ash had lived most of his adult life without his family. At least she'd had the good fortune to have hers around much longer. "Don't you ever think about making amends with your father?"

"No. His only concern is his wealth, his title. But I assure you that I will not treat our child with such disregard."

Karen trusted Ash would treat their child with great care. "I still think you should try to talk to him. I mean, regardless of what he's done, I'm sure he still loves you. After all, you're his son."

"He has no real concept of love. I, too, have come to realize that it is better not to put too much stock on those emotions. I have preferred to live my life through logic."

Karen's hope began to fade, replaced by her own need for self-protection. "I guess love isn't all it's cracked up to be. Who needs it, right?" She did.

At first Karen thought she'd only imagined the sudden change in Ash when his hold seemed to loosen around her. But when he unexpectedly rolled onto his back, away from her, she knew she wasn't imagining it at all.

"Did you love him?" he asked.

"My father?"

"Your ex-fiancé."

Karen thought she had at one time but obviously she'd been mistaken. She'd never entertained the same feelings for Carl that she now had for Ash. Feelings she had best put aside. "I think my relationship with him had as much to do with convenience as caring, although I did believe I cared for him at one time. We lived in a small town with few prospects and at the time I thought he was offering a good deal. But when I finally realized he wanted to own me, I backed out."

"In what way did he try to own you?"

"I wanted to open my own design business and he preferred that I stay home and be a rancher's wife. I couldn't live with a man who ignored my dreams."

Another stretch of silence suspended the conversation until Ash finally asked, "What dreams do you have, Karen?"

At least he had bothered to ask. Carl never had. "I want to have a happy, healthy child." *I want you to love me.* The thought vaulted into Karen's brain and only then did she realize how much she wanted his love. But if Ash had closed himself off to the possibility, chances were that wasn't going to happen.

"How about you?" she asked, trying not to sound too dejected. "What dreams do you have?"

"I prefer to think of them as goals, not dreams. Many I have already obtained in business. I hope to provide a stable home for our child, with two parents who work together to make certain that happens."

The response was almost void of emotion, and Karen's hope died completely. He hadn't said he wanted more than a partnership. He hadn't even hinted at love.

Karen rested one arm over her eyes and tried to fight back the tears for the second time tonight. Then to her surprise, Ash picked up her hand resting at her side and twined his fingers with hers. He lifted it to his lips for a gentle kiss then said, "May you have pleasant dreams tonight, Karen."

She wouldn't, that much she knew, because the dream

of having a real marriage, something she had never thought to consider when he had entered her life, was starting to disappear.

''Are you Karen Saalem?''

For the second time in as many days, Karen again confronted a stranger only this time the stranger stood at her front door and happened to be a man. A tall, lean man, strikingly handsome with shocking blue eyes that contrasted with his dark hair. He wore a tailored navy suit and a stoic expression that said he meant business. Since Karen didn't recognize him, she automatically assumed he was there to see Ash. But Ash had left that morning for a few appointments, so the guy was out of luck. After Ash's declarations last night, Karen feared so was she.

''If you're looking for my husband, he's not available at the moment.''

''I'm here to see you.''

Karen frowned. ''Okay. And you are?''

''Steven Conti.''

Great. Just what Karen needed this morning—Maria's lover on her doorstep probably armed with questions she wasn't prepared to answer. She gave him a polite smile instead of offering her hand. He didn't look as if he was in the mood for pleasantries. ''What can I do for you?''

He rubbed his neck with one palm and released a harsh, weary sigh. ''I need to speak with you about Maria.''

As she'd suspected. Karen considered telling him she was busy but decided there wasn't any use putting off the inevitable. Besides, he looked as if he could use a good listener, and that was all she intended to do—listen.

Karen stepped aside and gestured toward the foyer. ''Come in.'' After leading him into the living room, she pulled the drop cloth from the sofa and said, "Have a seat."

"I don't want to sit," he said. "I want to know where Maria is."

She faced him and wrung her hands. "Maria is on vacation."

"I don't believe it. I suspect her family found out about our relationship and sent her away to prevent us from being together."

At least Karen could tell him this much. "That's not true, Steven. Maria left of her own accord."

"Then you know where she is."

She hated that she had to withhold the truth, considering his obvious distress. But her vow of secrecy to Maria took precedence over his problems. "I promise she's safe. She needed some time to think things through. That's all."

"I have to know where she is. I have to talk to her."

"I can't tell you that. I promised Maria I wouldn't."

He forked his fingers through his dark hair and pinned Karen with angry eyes. "What about me? Do you think it's fair that she left me only a note without any explanation other than she needed time away?"

The abject pain in his voice cut Karen's heart to the quick. "It doesn't matter what I think. I have to respect Maria's wishes."

"Whether you tell me or not, I'm going to find her, no matter how long it takes. But you could make it easier on me by telling me where she is now."

"I wish I could, but I can't."

Steven clasped Karen's arms and she saw up close and personal the extent of his anguish. "I'm asking you to please reconsider. I'm asking you to have some compassion."

"And I am asking you to unhand my wife."

Steven dropped his hands and they both turned to see Ash standing in the den's entrance, his arms folded across his chest. Dressed in a suit and the traditional *kaffiyeh,* he looked formally businesslike, except for the menacing glare aimed at both Karen and Steven.

Steven put up his hands, palms forward. "Look, I don't want to cause any trouble here. I have enough of my own." He pulled a card from his jacket pocket and handed it to Karen. "Call me if you change your mind."

Steven brushed past Ash on his way out of the room, muttering "Sorry" and leaving Karen alone to face Ash's anger, and her own.

When she heard the front door close, she turned that anger on Ash. "What was that all about?"

"I believe I should be asking that question. What is your relationship with that man?"

"It doesn't involve you."

He took a step forward. "I see a stranger with his hands on my wife and this does not involve me?"

Karen braced her hands on her hips. "Do you really think I'd let some stranger into the house?"

"If he's not a stranger, then who is he?"

She had no choice but to tell him. "Steven Conti, Maria's lover."

Ash didn't seem all that shocked by the revelation but he definitely seemed angry. "What did he want with you?"

"He wanted me to tell him Maria's location, which, of course, I couldn't because of my promise to Maria. So you can just calm down."

"How was I to know that he was not threatening you?"

Karen released a bark of a laugh. "If you hadn't been

so determined to jump to conclusions, you would have noticed that Steven is in a lot of pain. He's totally lost without Maria.''

Ash's features softened, but only slightly. ''I only know that I saw some strange man with his hands on my wife.''

''Well, now you know the truth.'' Karen tossed the card onto the end table and the drop cloth back over the sofa. ''I don't appreciate you storming in here like some superhero determined to come to my rescue.''

''When I came upon you, I could only consider that—'' He looked away. ''It does not matter.''

Karen experienced a sharp sense of awareness and a little nip of satisfaction. ''Were you jealous, Sheikh Saalem?''

His gaze zipped back to her. ''Jealousy is an imprudent emotion. My concern was with your safety.''

''I suppose you could be right. You didn't seem at all jealous the other night over the prospect that some sailor could be watching us make love.''

His eyes went dark as midnight. ''That was only fantasy, Karen. Had I known that some man had seen you naked, I would have been tempted to do him bodily harm.''

''Oh, really?'' She folded her arms and smiled. ''And you're not jealous? I suppose that would be beneath a strong, emotionless prince like yourself.''

He raked the *kaffiyeh* from his head and hurled it across the room. ''I reacted as a man, not as a prince.''

''A man who was concerned with his wife's safety, I know.'' Karen strolled to the club chair, sat and pulled her legs beneath her. ''Of course, any normal husband might be a little jealous considering that Steven Conti is a very attractive man. But since this marriage is in name only, I certainly understand why that wouldn't enter your mind.''

Ash took a stalking step forward. ''What do you want from me, Karen?''

''The truth.''

''What truth?''

''That you wondered if maybe I had taken another lover, unlike the sea captain's devoted wife. That maybe you had some doubts that you haven't been giving me everything I need so I decided to turn to someone else.''

He braced his hands on the chair's arms on either side of Karen. ''Have you not found my attentions satisfactory?''

''You've been a very considerate lover.''

''Considerate?'' Ash leaned closer, only inches from her mouth. The tension hung thick between them, their eyes locked together and their bodies in close proximity. ''Obviously I have failed if that is how you wish to describe our lovemaking. Perhaps I should endeavor to prove to you that I am capable of more than consideration.''

Karen knew all too well that if she threw down the proverbial gauntlet, Ash would be more than willing to take it up. Maybe there wasn't much wisdom in that considering what he'd told her last night, but she couldn't deny that she still wanted him in a very elemental way, even if she couldn't have his love. ''Go ahead, prove it.''

He pushed away from the chair. ''I would be glad to prove it if I were assured you were feeling up to it.''

Karen glanced at his now distended fly. ''Obviously you are quite *up* to it.''

''My current condition does not take precedence over yours.''

She sent him a challenging look. ''I'm personally feeling quite well.'' She pulled the sweatshirt over her head and tossed it onto the floor, leaving her clad in a black lace bra and jeans. ''Do you care to find out for yourself how I'm feeling?''

Karen saw the indecision as well as the desire in his eyes, but he remained motionless. At least he hadn't run away.

After slowly lowering the zipper, she wriggled out of her jeans and dropped them on the floor to join her sweatshirt. She felt really, really wicked and very determined to get his attention through whatever means necessary. She decided she did have his attention when he visually followed the movement as she traced the lace band below her navel with a fingertip. ''Are you absolutely, positively sure you're not interested?''

Ash tore his jacket away and sent it sailing across the room, startling her. Karen wasn't surprised when he pulled her up into his arms, expecting him to carry her into the bedroom. She didn't expect him to seat her on the drop-cloth-covered sofa and yank her panties away. And she definitely wasn't prepared when he fell to his knees, parted her legs and began a sensual assault with his mouth.

With every pass of his soft, abrading tongue over her susceptible center, Karen felt as if she might fall into some carnal abyss, never to return. With every slide of his finger deep inside her, she came closer and closer to calling out from the sheer pleasure of it all. But she didn't dare stop him, nor could she halt the explosive climax that claimed her with steady waves of pure bliss.

Ash rose and stared down at her with eyes as intense as his intimate kiss. ''Was I *considerate* enough?''

Karen took a few moments to catch her breath. ''Oh, yes, very considerate.'' She came to her knees and tugged away his belt then lowered his zipper. ''But it seems to me that you could use a little consideration, too.''

After she freed him, Karen let go of her inhibitions and took him into her mouth. He molded her scalp with his large palms and let her explore his length with her lips, her tongue, but only for a short time before he framed her head in his hands and pulled her away.

''Enough.''

She looked up at him with a grin. ''Are you sure?''

''No.'' He joined her on the sofa in a rush and after kicking his slacks and briefs away he took her down onto the cushions and entered her with a deep thrust.

He kissed her thoroughly as he moved inside her in an erotic tempo. He fondled her breasts through the lace of her bra then suckled her through the fabric. It was as if they fed each other, consumed by a desire that knew no limits. As if the passion between them took on a life of its own and nothing could prevent it from taking control.

Ash braced his palms on either side of her and rose up on straightened arms, taking most of his weight from her. ''Am I being considerate enough?''

''You're doing okay.'' But she wasn't at all okay. She ached for him, ached from a love that she hadn't welcomed at all. She tugged him back into her arms, against her sprinting heart, as the steady pace he had kept took an almost frantic turn.

Karen was vaguely aware of the sound of a truck's engine shutting down, the opening and closing of doors. Realization that the work crew had arrived only heightened the tension. ''Hurry,'' she said in a harsh whisper.

He raised his head, his face showing the strain of his impending climax. ''No.''

''The workers are here and I unlocked the—''

Ash cut off her words with another electrifying kiss

and again Karen was lost, not caring who might find them, not caring about anything but Ash's powerful body and his remarkable stamina.

When she heard the back door open, Ash brought her legs around his waist, touched her again and she came completely apart. He buried his face in her neck and shuddered forcefully in her arms.

The sound of footsteps forced Karen back into reality. At least the louvered doors to the kitchen were closed, affording some privacy. She worked her way from beneath Ash, grabbed her jeans and sweatshirt from the floor but after a harried visual search couldn't find her underwear. Figuring some clothes were better than none, she yanked on her pants and shirt.

"Are you looking for these?"

Karen glanced up to find Ash dangling her black lace panties from one finger. She snatched them from his hand and stuffed them into her back pocket. "Get dressed," she hissed. "They're liable to come in here at any moment."

Ash looked over his shoulder toward the opening leading to the kitchen. "If they do not have the decency to knock, then my state of undress should not come as any surprise."

Karen almost smiled as she studied his state of undress, the now totally wrinkled tailored shirt covering him from the thighs up, his tie hanging askew, his dark, thick hair a total mess. He looked sexy as hell, but this was no time for Karen to stand and gawk at him.

She grabbed his pants and briefs from the floor and flung them at him. "Put these on. You might not be concerned with your reputation, but I have to work with these guys."

Ash complied, slowly rising from the sofa, taking his

sweet time putting his slacks back on. Karen adjusted her clothing, pulled a cloth band from her pocket and piled her hair into a ponytail.

Although they were now somewhat presentable, Karen assumed that if anyone happened to come into the room he would immediately know what had transpired only moments before by the guilt on her face.

Then the foolishness of what she had done bit into her. She'd given in to her own needs, his sensual lure, knowing what it would do to her emotionally. What it would continue to do to her if she kept allowing it to happen. She had to remember that this had nothing to do with love, at least on Ash's part. Had to remember that every time he made love to her, he staked a claim to another piece of her heart and soon there would be nothing left.

"This is not supposed to be this way between us," Karen muttered.

Ash paused from tucking his shirt into his waistband. "How is it supposed to be?"

"We said we were going to keep this relationship platonic."

"You said as much, Karen, not me. And what of the other night when you claimed we would share in more of these moments?"

"I've changed my mind." He had changed it when he'd told her he was incapable of loving again. "I shouldn't be asking you anymore."

He stepped forward and took her hands into his. "Yet you keep asking me. Am I wrong for answering you? Am I to be strong enough for us both?"

She had been wrong to start believing that maybe he was able to love her. Wrong to believe that more could exist between them beyond passion.

Karen pulled her hands from his. "You're right. It is

my fault. But our intimacy only complicates everything. It's important to me to stay in control of my life.''

''I have no intention of owning you, Karen, unlike your ex-fiancé. I only want to take care of you and our child.''

Again he'd failed to mention having any feelings for her. ''I don't need to be protected.'' *I need your love.* ''And this isn't just about my relationship with Carl. A few months ago my whole life was totally out of control. I can't let that happen again.''

''You continue to misjudge my motives. Everything I have done has been out of concern for your welfare.''

But not because of his love for her, Karen realized. ''We need to remember that we both entered into this arrangement knowing it wouldn't be permanent.''

''So you believe,'' he murmured as he moved across the room, picked up his jacket and folded it over one arm. ''Then perhaps we should begin acting as if that were the case. I cannot do that with you in my bed. I am not that strong.''

He turned and headed toward the exit, then faced her again, some unnamed emotion reflecting from his dark eyes. ''I will arrange to have a bedroom suite delivered tomorrow. I will leave you with your celibacy. I will also expect you to leave me with mine.''

In other words, don't touch me, Karen thought. She felt as if she'd been pummeled about the head and heart even though she realized it would be best to keep her distance, physically and emotionally.

''Fine,'' she said with confidence, although she felt as if she were dying inside. ''If you'd prefer to sleep in another room, I won't bother you.''

''I prefer that you—'' He looked away. ''It does not

matter. You have already decided what will be.'' He spun on his heels and walked away.

Karen laid her hand on her abdomen, the place that sheltered her unborn child, trying to remember why she had agreed to this arrangement in the first place. When she and Ash parted ways, at least she would have her baby. A baby that would bind them for years.

Had she made a mistake? No. Regardless of how desperately she hurt inside, she would never regret having him in her life, having him as her baby's father. She would probably always regret that she hadn't been strong enough not to love him.

Later that evening, Karen climbed into bed, alone. She'd spent most of the morning meeting with the contractor and workers who were nearing completion on the kitchen. Next they would move on to the nursery, as soon as she selected the wall coverings from the samples she'd obtained earlier in the week.

She wanted to include Ash in the process but since their earlier encounter, he'd gone to his office and hadn't come out except to grab a plate of food to take back upstairs with him. Several times she'd stood outside his office door, preparing to ask him if he'd like to be involved in the decorating decisions. But each time she'd been poised to knock, pride made her pull away. He'd said he didn't want to be bothered, and she needed to respect that no matter how badly it hurt.

On the brink of a good cry, Karen decided she could use something to distract her, a friendly voice. A friend. Besides, she needed to tell Maria about Steven's surprise visit. She also hadn't spoken to her cousin since she'd called and told her about the baby several days ago and her absence from work.

After snatching the phone from its cradle, Karen dialed the Calderones' number, hoping Maria might answer. She loved Louis and Magdalene, but both could talk the kernels off a corncob. Karen wasn't in the mood to answer any questions, and knowing the couple as she did, either one would sense something was terribly wrong, then she'd spend the evening playing twenty questions.

As luck would have it, Maria did answer on the second ring, "Calderone residence."

"So how are things in the great state of Montana?" She sounded falsely cheerful, even to her own ears.

"Karen! It's so great to hear your voice."

"Yours, too." Karen bit her lip to thwart a sob. "How are you feeling?"

"Pregnant," Maria said. "Lonely."

"I know the feeling."

"Uh-oh. You sound depressed."

"I'm a little blue."

"Want to talk about it?"

"That's partly why I'm calling, but first I wanted to tell you that Mimi has everything under control at Baronessa. I've been in touch with her by phone several times."

"As I told you before, Karen, I understand you need some time off. Mimi's been around a long time. She can handle things in our absence."

"I really appreciate that, Maria." Now for the hard part. "Second, I need to tell you something that involves your situation."

"The family knows where I am." Maria's voice held an edge of panic.

"Not the family. At least not that I'm aware of. But it could be only a matter of time before Steven does."

"How?"

''He paid me a visit, but I promise I told him nothing other than that you'd left by choice. He thought someone in the family found out about you two and shipped you off.''

''Did he say anything else?''

''Only that he'd find you, no matter how long it takes.''

Maria's dejected sigh filtered through the phone line. ''I can't stop him if he tries. Maybe he'll give up before that happens.''

''Are you sure you don't want him to find you?''

''I don't know what I want anymore. Don't get me wrong, the Calderones have been wonderful. I only thought that being here might help me sort things through but I'm still confused.''

Karen could definitely relate. ''I hope you get everything squared away soon. Steven is really hurting.''

''I know. But I still have so much to consider.''

''So do I. Obviously this confusion must be the result of a full moon or a family thing since I'm in the same boat.''

''Then this mood of yours has to do with you and Ash.''

''You could say that.''

''You're in love with him, aren't you?''

Karen should be shocked by Maria's uncanny knack at reading her so well, but she wasn't. ''Yes, like an idiot, I've totally fallen for him.''

''That's wonderful, Karen.'' Maria sounded sincerely happy.

''No, it's not.''

''Why?''

''Because he can never feel the same about me.''

''He told you that?'' Now Maria sounded shocked.

"Not in so many words, but he had a bad experience with another woman and he's decided he doesn't have any use for those emotions. Neither did I, until I met him."

"People do change, Karen."

"I'd love to believe that, but Ash is very set in his ways. And he's so infuriatingly protective where I'm concerned. You know how I feel about that."

"Yes, I know, and you need to stop and consider that maybe your history with Carl is coloring your judgment. Maybe Ash's feelings for you directly relate to him wanting to take care of you. You know how men can be. Voicing those feelings doesn't always come easily for them. My guess is that you're both too proud to come clean."

Could that be the case? Could Ash be fighting his feelings for her, too? That was almost unfathomable. "You could be right, but I'm too scared too hope."

"Love is a very scary business, Karen. Someone has to make the first move."

Meaning her, Karen decided. "I've really thought about telling him how I feel, but we had an argument this morning and he's angry with me. I basically told him that I didn't want any more intimacy between us. He hasn't spoken to me since."

"Oh, Karen. I know this is tough, but maybe you should choke down some of that Barone pride and let him know you've fallen in love with him. What's the worst thing that could happen?"

"He could reject me. I don't think I can take that."

"Are you sure he doesn't think you've rejected him?"

Karen had rejected Ash in many ways. Rejected his concern for her, rejected her feelings for him, or at least she'd tried—unsuccessfully. The tears began to roll down her cheeks in a steady stream, but she spoke around them with effort. ''You're probably right, Maria. I just don't know what to do next.''

''I'll tell you what you need to do. Go out tomorrow and buy a nice skimpy negligee and supplies for an intimate dinner for two, complete with candles. Make that meal, wear that gown, or nothing at all, then spill your guts.''

Karen laughed through her tears. ''Sounds like a plan. A good one.''

''Of course it is. You have the opportunity to spend your life with the man you love. Some people never have that.''

Feeling remorseful, Karen said, ''I believe you could have that, too, Maria. With Steven.''

''Don't worry about me. I only want you to make sure you don't squander the opportunity. As they say, nothing ventured, nothing gained.''

That suddenly seemed to make perfect sense to Karen. She had taken a risk coming to Boston. If she hadn't, she would have missed out on knowing Maria and her new family. She would have missed out on a new life. She might never have the baby she'd always wanted, and she definitely never would have met Ash—a man who would definitely be worth the risk.

She would tell him everything tomorrow night, tell him that she loved him, tell him that she wanted to make the marriage work. And maybe, just maybe, she might find that he did have feelings for her, too. If not, then she would make an effort to convince him that life wasn't as worthwhile without having someone to love—and being loved in return.

Ten

After spending a restless night on the downstairs sofa, Ash awoke to find Karen gone. She had left without telling him where she was going, without leaving some kind of note as to when she might return. In an irrational, blind panic, he rushed into the bedroom, thankfully discovering that her belongings still remained. He called Baronessa but no one there had seen her or expected to see her. Last, he contacted the doctor's office to learn that she wasn't scheduled to come in for another month.

He then began to worry that she was searching for a new place to reside while he sat alone in his office, pondering how his pride and fear could have cost him the most important person in his life.

Yesterday he'd had the perfect opportunity to state his case. Instead, he had given in to a desire for Karen that knew no bounds. He had escaped before he had told her that a life without her would mean much less to him. But he'd also recalled their conversation two nights ago when she'd said she had no need for love, and then yesterday when she had told him she no longer wanted his attention.

Yet he wondered if perhaps she was afraid as well. He suspected she feared that he would try to control her life. In reality, she was very much in control of his. She commanded his every waking moment, his every thought, and now, though he had waged a battle against it, she had slipped past the barrier he had so carefully built around his emotions. He could no longer deny that he felt much more than fondness for Karen.

Ash refused to give up on their marriage. If she could not believe that he respected her individuality, her independence, everything she was as a woman, lover and friend, he would simply have to prove it.

He needed more time to think things through yet he did not have that luxury. He had a busy schedule beginning in less than an hour, two appointments involving important clients. What was more important, business or his wife?

His wife. A few months ago he would never have considered rearranging his agenda for anyone unless an absolute emergency had arisen. A few weeks ago, he had lived a desolate life, or so it now seemed. Now that he realized how very much he loved his wife.

As far as he was concerned, his current dilemma—finding some way to prove himself to Karen—definitely qualified as an emergency. He would cancel the appointments. He would find some means to demonstrate how much she meant to him, even if it took all day. Even if it took the rest of his life.

Even if he was forced to give Karen her freedom.

* * *

Karen returned from the market midafternoon with her arms full of groceries and her heart heavy with dread. She'd left early that morning before Ash had awakened, before she had to face him. She wasn't quite ready to do that yet.

After she slipped the roast into the oven, she went upstairs to make sure he wasn't home, although his car hadn't been in the drive. She knocked on his office door and when she didn't get a response opened it to find the room deserted. She walked back toward the stairs and noticed the door was open to the guest room at the end of the corridor. Odd since that particular room had remained closed off, awaiting renovations. Surely Ash wasn't hiding out in there. On the off chance he was, Karen headed down the hall to investigate.

She didn't find Ash in the room but she did find furniture, a stark bedroom suite made of pine with a lone dresser and a bare, queen-size mattress. Her heart took a dive when she realized Ash had done what he'd said he would do—prepared a place for himself to sleep, a place that didn't include her. But hadn't she told him that was fine?

It wasn't fine. Not in the least. She wanted him in her bed—*their* bed—and if her plan worked, maybe she would have him there tonight.

On that thought, she hurried down the stairs and practically sprinted through the living room where one worker stood on a ladder, applying molding to the ceiling.

Karen glanced up at him for only a second but it was enough to distract her from skirting the furniture moved helter-skelter about the room. Before she realized what was happening, her foot tangled in a drop cloth and she tumbled down to her knees. She rolled onto her back and a groan escaped her parted lips, more out of fear than the sharp, stinging pain in her ankle.

Closing her eyes tightly, she said a silent prayer for her unborn child as she laid a palm on her belly. At least she hadn't landed flat on her face. She didn't have any other pain aside from her ankle and hoped upon hope she hadn't done any real damage beyond a minor sprain. As she tried to sit up, a hand on her shoulder stopped her. She opened her eyes to the man who'd been on the ladder, an older gentleman with silver hair and a smile that reminded her of her father.

"Are you okay, lady?" he asked.

"I think so. I'm pregnant, so I'm a little worried."

He shook his head. "Sheesh, that's not good. Maybe I should take you to the hospital to get you checked out."

"I think you're right. I should probably go to the hospital. You'll find a number on the refrigerator beneath a magnet. It says 'Daniel and Phoebe.' If you call them, they'll come and take me."

"Are you sure? It wouldn't be a problem to drive you myself."

She didn't like the idea of getting in a car with a stranger, even one who seemed nice. But she did want to make certain everything was okay with the baby. "I appreciate your offer, but my cousin and his wife wouldn't mind taking me."

"Okay. If you're sure."

The man left for the kitchen while Karen hoped and prayed for Phoebe or Daniel to be home. Hoped that they hadn't changed their plans and left for their second honeymoon before next week. Her prayers were answered when the workman returned and reported that Phoebe was on her way.

Karen probably should call Ash on his cell phone but

more than likely he had it turned off, his usual practice while in a business meeting. She didn't want to leave a message on his voice mail saying she was en route to the hospital. It would be better if she reported to him after she was sure nothing was broken and the baby was fine. He would only worry himself sick. Still, she needed him more than ever now, needed his comfort, needed him to tell her it would all be okay. But if things didn't work out between them, she would again have to rely only on herself.

Ash tore into the house, not knowing at all what to expect. Daniel had left him a message on his voice mail stating that Karen had injured her ankle but was otherwise fine after a visit to the hospital emergency room. Ash wanted to believe that was the case. Yet he doubted Daniel would have told him if something was more seriously wrong with Karen or their child.

He strode into the living room to find Daniel seated on the sofa. "Where is she?"

Daniel rose and said, "Slow down there, Ash. She's in the bedroom with Phoebe. She's okay."

Ash clutched the paper bag in his fist, resisting the urge to tear it to shreds out of anger and frustration. "Why did she not call me?"

Daniel slipped his hands into his pockets. "You'll have to ask her, but I'm guessing she didn't want to worry you. Maybe she was afraid of your reaction. Considering you rushed in here like a raging bull, maybe she was justified."

"Of course I'm concerned. She's my wife. She's carrying my child. She's everything—" *To me.*

Daniel gave him a significant look. "It seems this little marriage arrangement between you two has taken a surprising turn.'' He paced in front of the sofa, occasionally glancing at Ash now and then. ''Yeah, it looks as if the sheikh has finally met his match.''

Ash didn't appreciate Daniel's goading though he recognized the truth in his friend's words. He had met his match in Karen. A perfect match. If only he could convince her of that.

Phoebe walked into the room carrying a tray containing a bowl and a half-full glass of milk. ''Did an unexpected storm happen to come through the house? The slamming door rattled the walls.''

Daniel presented a wry grin. ''No storm, just the sheikh looking for his wife.''

Phoebe nodded toward the corridor leading to the master suite. ''She's tucked away in bed. I think she could use some company.''

But would she want his company? Ash decided she was going to have it whether she wanted it or not. ''Then she's doing well? The baby—''

''They're fine,'' Phoebe said. ''It's only an ankle sprain, nothing broken, no other damage done. If fact, she's wide-awake and stir-crazy. She wanted to get out of bed and finish making dinner for you but I wouldn't let her.''

Dinner? Was that to be the last meal before her departure? ''I am very relieved to know she has limited injuries, and I'm very grateful to you both.''

''No problem,'' Daniel said.

Phoebe stared toward the kitchen and halted then faced Ash again. ''I can fix you a plate of food if you'd like. Karen made a very nice roast.''

The last thing Ash desired was food. He needed to see about his wife. ''That is not necessary. Please make yourself comfortable, or if you wish, you may return home now. I will handle the situation from here.''

Daniel's grin deepened. ''I'm sure you'll handle everything fine. Just remember Karen has a bum ankle, so you're going to have to be careful while you're doing the handling.''

''Daniel, behave,'' Phoebe scolded. ''I'll just put this away, Ash, and then we'll get out of your hair.''

Ash thanked the heavens for Phoebe's common sense. ''Again, I'm in your debt.''

Daniel offered his hand for a shake. ''And believe me, I'll find a way to collect. I've been studying the markets—''

''You're incorrigible, Daniel Barone,'' Phoebe said with amusement as she walked into the kitchen.

''And you love me for it,'' Daniel called out to his wife.

''I suppose you wouldn't mind seeing yourselves out as I see to Karen.'' Ash normally wouldn't be such a poor host, especially in light of his friends' assistance, but he wasn't willing to wait another moment before he was at Karen's side.

''Go ahead,'' Daniel said. ''I'm sure she's eager to see you, too.''

If only that were true, Ash thought as he walked down the hallway toward the bedroom. He paused outside the door to gather his thoughts and muster his courage. Although he despised the thought of her being in pain, even if only a minor discomfort, perhaps the accident had bought him more time. She could not very well leave if she could not walk. At the moment he could probably use a miracle.

He slowly opened the door to find Karen reclining

against a pillow, and another one bolstering her ankle that had been wrapped like a turban.

When she looked up, Ash noted the surprise in her hazel eyes, perhaps even joy. Or perhaps he only wanted to see that so badly he was imagining its existence.

He set the paper bag on the dresser and approached the bed, pausing to look upon her injured ankle. "Is there much discomfort?"

"A little," she said. "I'm just thankful that I didn't do more damage. I was afraid..."

When tears welled in her eyes, Ash sat on the edge of the bed at her side. He wanted to hold her, to assure her that everything would be all right, that he would make certain of it, but he did not want to do anything that she would not welcome. He settled for taking her hand.

"I am sorry for not being here for you, Karen," he began. "I am also sorry that you felt you could not call me."

She wiped her free hand over her damp eyes. "That wasn't it. I didn't want to worry you until I knew everything was okay. That's why Daniel called you from the emergency room after the exam."

"Then everything is all right?" He needed her personal pledge, despite Daniel and Phoebe's assurances.

"Yes, everything is fine, as far as our baby is concerned." She studied their joined hands. "But everything isn't fine as far as we're concerned."

"You have decided to leave before our child's birth."

Her gaze came to rest on his, reflecting confusion. "Leave?"

"When I realized you'd left this morning without waking me, I assumed you were probably searching for a place to live."

"Ash, you assumed wrong. I went shopping. I'd

planned to have a nice dinner and, afterward, a chance for us to talk. To really talk. I have something I need to tell you.''

Ash experienced a momentary rush of relief then a good portion of concern when he considered that what she needed to tell him might not be what he wanted to hear. ''I have something that I need to say to you as well.''

Her hand tensed in his. ''Okay.''

''Perhaps you should go first,'' he said.

''No, you go first.''

''All right, I will.'' He brought her hand to his lips and kissed it softly. ''What I am about to say to you will probably be the most difficult message I have ever tried to convey, so I will ask for your patience.''

''I'm listening.''

He shifted on the bed to face her fully in an effort to gauge her reaction. ''For many years, I believed I had a satisfying existence. I had my business, my friends, my freedom, my title. But I did not have the very thing that makes one truly feel alive, until you came into my life.''

He touched her face and wiped away a tear with his thumb. ''You were everything I feared, a woman who had the means to tear away the wall I have built, unearthing emotions I have never welcomed. I saw it as a weakness, yet in you I have found a strength I never knew I possessed.''

He paused to say the words he had never thought to say again to any woman. ''You asked me once about my dreams, my wishes. You are all those things, Karen. You have made me whole again.''

Her tears came full force now, tearing at Ash's heart. ''Oh, God.''

He let go of her hand, believing he would be forced

to let her go as well. ''I am sorry to cause you more pain, but this is how I feel. I respect your decision if you want to adhere to our original terms. If you still wish to leave, I will not stop you. I would rather spend my life alone than spend it with someone who is not with me of her own free will, even if I do love her with everything that I am.''

She sniffed and brought his palm to rest against her cheek. ''You're so wrong, Ash. I'm not having any pain, and I'm not going anywhere.''

He frowned. ''I do not understand.''

''It's very simple, really. I've been the same as you, closing myself off out of fear of losing control of my life. But the truth is, with you I'm finally starting to feel that my life makes perfect sense. In other words, I love you, too.''

She might as well have offered him the key to heaven considering the lightness in his heart. ''You do?''

''Yes, and I've probably loved you since the moment I found you sitting naked in the hotel. Maybe even from that first moment you kissed me. I was too afraid to tell you. But I'm not afraid anymore.''

He brushed a kiss across her lips, finding them warm and inviting. ''It seems we have both been living in a house built on pride.''

She wrapped her arms around his neck and pulled him closer. ''Yes, we have, but I think it's time we tear that house down.''

''As do I.'' He kissed her fully then, with the love he had fought so hard not to claim. He could not deny the fire the kiss incited within him, but he had to consider her current condition, and that he had more to offer beyond making love to her.

Pulling away, he said, ''I have something for you. A special gift. Actually, three gifts.''

"I don't know how you're going to top what you've already given me, a baby and a future."

"I would hope that you would allow me to try." He came to his feet and walked to the dresser to retrieve the bag he'd discarded upon entering the room.

When he returned to Karen's side, she eyed the sack with blatant curiosity. "Did you bring me a bagel? I've really been wanting a bagel."

He pulled the jar from the bag. "Olives. But I see you have changed cravings without my knowledge."

She laughed. "I still want the olives *and* the bagel."

"I will see to the bagels later." He set the jar on the nightstand and fished the key from his pocket then placed it in her hand. "And this is for you as well."

She held the key up to the light. "Did you buy another house?"

"Not a house. A building near Baronessa. I've purchased it for you."

"What would I need with a building?"

He reclaimed his seat on the bed. "You will probably need only part of the building; the remaining offices can be leased out. But I believe the bottom floor will suit your interior design establishment quite well. If it is not to your liking, then I will sell it and buy you another."

Her mouth dropped open and her eyes widened. "You've bought me my own business?"

"I have bought you the location. It will be up to you to develop it. With your permission, I would like to handle the financial aspects."

"Of course. Math is definitely not my thing. But I'm not sure I should even try this until after the baby is born. Maybe not until the baby's older."

"You will have access to many rooms. One you can prepare as an on-site nursery so you will have our child with you. If you so desire, we can hire an au pair, as long as you choose a female. I do not like the thought of my wife spending time with a houseboy.''

She pulled him into another embrace before pulling away to say, ''I don't need a houseboy when I have you.''

He stood again and reached deeper into his pocket to retrieve the final purchase. ''I have saved the most important gift for last, to prove that you will always have me.''

He handed Karen the gold band and she held it up much the same as she had the key. ''Ash, I'm not sure about this one. It looks too big. Besides, I already have a ring. A beautiful ring.''

''It is for me, Karen. A symbol that I am truly your husband and that this marriage is real in every sense. If that is how you wish it to be.''

''That's the only way I want it to be.'' With another rush of tears, Karen lifted his hand and slipped the ring on his finger. She looked up at him with a love that he, too, felt soul-deep. ''This means so very much to me. And you know what else I would like?''

''Anything.''

She nodded toward the journal she kept at her bedside. ''It took too many years for me to know my true heritage. Don't let that happen to our child. Forgive your father and ask him to be a part of our baby's life. Our lives.''

So much she was asking of him, but for Karen he would put aside his past. ''I will call him first thing in the morning, but I make no guarantees he will speak to me.''

She pulled him back down beside her. ''Maria told me recently that people change, Ash. She was right.''

How well he knew. "You have most definitely changed me with your love."

Her eyes misted again. "We've changed each other, for the better. Which leads me to another bit of unfinished business."

She reached around him, opened the drawer in the nightstand and handed him a bundle of papers. "Here."

He unfolded the document, discovering it to be the original agreement they had signed prior to their wedding. "What do you wish me to do with these?"

"I want to rip them up in little pieces."

"I would like nothing better."

Yet before Ash could make even the slightest tear, Karen said, "Wait."

"You have changed your mind?"

"No." She worked her way off the bed, sliding her feet to the floor. "I want you to throw them into the ocean, and I want to watch."

"You should not be walking on your injured ankle."

She smiled. "I know that. You'll have to carry me."

"Gladly." After slipping the document into his pocket, he picked Karen up and carried her onto the porch.

When he set her on the wall's ledge, she said, "Hold on to me, Ash. The last thing I need is to take another fall."

Ash had taken his own fall into love with her, a fall he would never regret. He tightened his arms around her and softly kissed her lips. "You may rest assured that I will never let you go."

"And you may rest assured that I'm not going to let you let me go. You're stuck with me." To prove that fact, Karen took the papers from his shirt pocket and shredded them into tiny little pieces, tossing them over her shoulder the way her mother had tossed the salt when she'd spilled it from the shaker, for luck. Who needed luck in the presence of love?

After she was finished, Karen wiped her palms together then placed her hands on Ash's wide shoulders. "Now you know what else I need?"

"A bath?"

She grinned. "You're on the right track." She opened her robe and held it out like wings, letting the cold ocean breeze ride over her bare skin, her laughter floating out to sea along with all of her former fears of letting go.

"You are not playing fair," Ash said, his eyes darkened to the color of night. "My hands are not free."

Karen felt remarkably free, totally liberated. "You don't have to use your hands, you know."

"An astute observation." He rested his lips in the valley between her breasts, but before he could work his wonders on her, he lifted his head and met her gaze. "You know where this will lead. In light of your injury—"

"I feel great, so stop worrying." Karen framed his beautiful face in her palms. "Ash, I want to make love with you knowing that's what we're doing, really making love." She painted kisses over his cheek. "Besides, I'm sure a creative guy like yourself can manage it. After all, you've said there are many ways to make love. I want you to show me."

"I would be happy to show you, but I believe we best do so in our bed. As I recall, we have yet to make love there."

Karen thought a minute. "You know, you're right. In fact, we haven't made love in several places, including your office. That should be next on our list. Do you think your desk will work?"

Ash laughed then, a low, deep laugh that resounded

with joy. "I fear I may never be gainfully employed again."

"I fear you may be right."

When Ash hoisted Karen from the ledge, she wrapped her legs around his waist and her arms around his neck as he carried her inside.

Ash set Karen in the middle of the bed, removed her robe and panties and gingerly propped her leg back on the pillow. As he undressed, she looked at him with wonder, studying every detail as if seeing him for the first time. In many ways it was a first, loving him so openly. She felt so very glad that she had given herself to him, as he had given himself to her.

Once he'd removed all his clothing, he came to her and took one pillow to place underneath her knees and another beneath her hips, careful not to disturb her ailing foot. For the longest moment he simply stared into her eyes before touching his lips to her ankle then moving between her parted legs to do the same to her belly, where he paused to say, "Our child is a testament to our love."

Karen laid a hand on his dark hair. "I couldn't agree more."

He whisked his hands over her flushed body and invited her to do the same with his. They spent lingering moments only touching, caressing, learning the intimate territories as if they had all the time in the world.

After Ash sent Karen spiraling into pleasure with a sweep of his hand and again with his persuasive mouth, he slid inside her so gracefully, so tenderly that Karen wanted to cry. And she did, shedding joyful tears as she realized she would never again be alone. She had her baby and the man who had made it all possible. The man who had so effectively captured her heart.

After they lay spent in each other's arms, Karen felt completely connected to Ash, not only through their joined bodies, not only through the child they had made, but also through a love she had never imagined.

Ash laid his head against her breast and told her, ''If there is anything I have failed to give you, you need only ask.''

Karen took his palm and laid it against her abdomen. ''You've given me this.'' Then she lifted his hand and placed it over his heart. ''And this. What more could I need?''

He showed her his love through his perfect smile and another perfect kiss. ''You will always have my love.''

Karen trusted his words to be true. She finally trusted herself. And most important, she trusted him. The father of her child. Her lover and partner in life.

Her husband—in the sweetest, truest sense of the word.

* * * * *

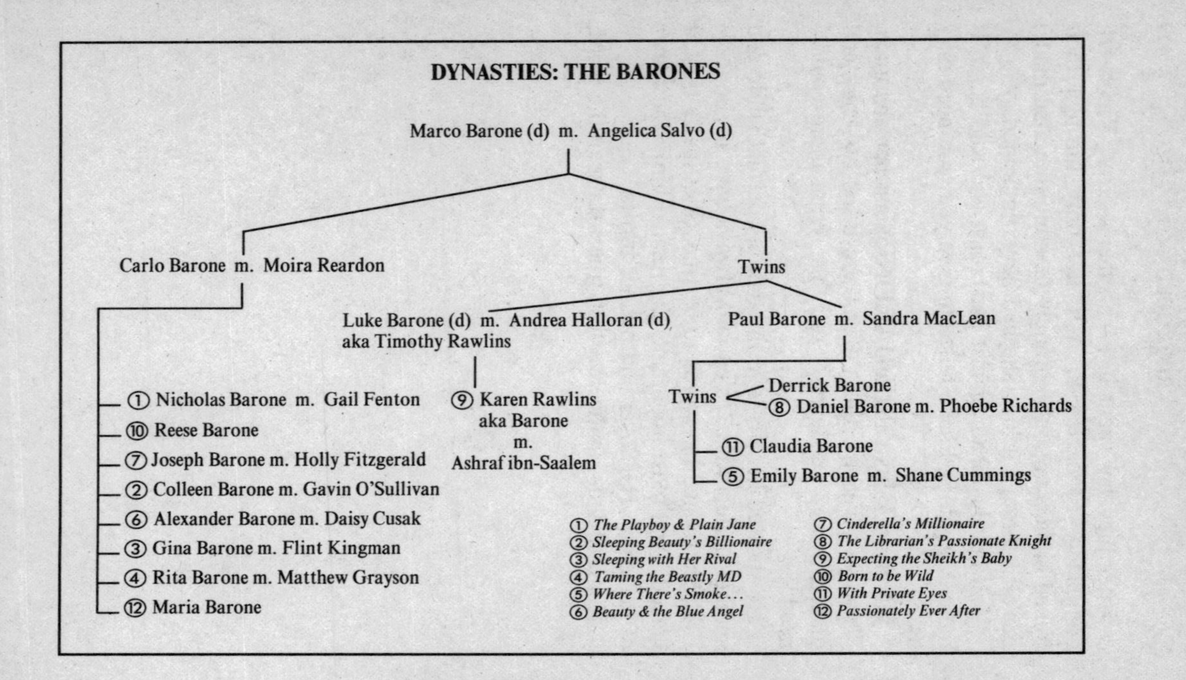
DYNASTIES: THE BARONES
Marco Barone (d) m. Angelica Salvo (d)
Carlo Barone m. Moira Reardon
Twins
Luke Barone (d) m. Andrea Halloran (d)
aka Timothy Rawlins
Paul Barone m. Sandra MacLean
① Nicholas Barone m. Gail Fenton
⑩ Reese Barone
⑦ Joseph Barone m. Holly Fitzgerald
② Colleen Barone m. Gavin O'Sullivan
⑥ Alexander Barone m. Daisy Cusak
③ Gina Barone m. Flint Kingman
④ Rita Barone m. Matthew Grayson
⑫ Maria Barone
⑨ Karen Rawlins
aka Barone
m.
Ashraf ibn-Saalem
Twins
Derrick Barone
⑧ Daniel Barone m. Phoebe Richards
⑪ Claudia Barone
⑤ Emily Barone m. Shane Cummings
① The Playboy & Plain Jane
② Sleeping Beauty's Billionaire
③ Sleeping with Her Rival
④ Taming the Beastly MD
⑤ Where There's Smoke…
⑥ Beauty & the Blue Angel
⑦ Cinderella's Millionaire
⑧ The Librarian's Passionate Knight
⑨ Expecting the Sheikh's Baby
⑩ Born to be Wild
⑪ With Private Eyes
⑫ Passionately Ever After

DYNASTIES: THE BARONES *continues...*
Turn the page for a bonus look at what's in store for you in the next Barones book—only from Silhouette Desire!

1538 BORN TO BE WILD

by Anne Marie Winston
October 2003

Prologue

"*S*he said *what?*" Twenty-one-year-old Reese Barone, seated in the parlor of his family home in Boston's Beacon Hill district, stared at his father in shock.

"Eliza Mayhew says that she's pregnant and you are the father." Carlo Barone stood before the elaborate marble fireplace, hands clasped behind his back. He eyed his second-to-eldest son sternly. "Needless to say, your mother and I are very disappointed in you, Reese."

"But I never—"

"Reese." His father's voice was colder than he'd ever heard it. "There will be no discussion. You will do the right thing and marry Ms. Mayhew at the end of the month."

"I will not." Reese leaped to his feet, nearly upsetting the elegant wing chair in which he'd been sitting while he'd waited to find out what could possibly have gotten his old man's drawers in such a twist. "That baby isn't mine."

On the love seat facing them, his mother Moira bowed her head as a sob escaped.

Carlo's face darkened with anger. "Haven't you already done enough to damage our family name?" he demanded. "First you get involved with that fisherman's daughter in Harwich—"

"There's nothing wrong with Celia," Reese said hotly, "except that she doesn't come with a pedigree."

"It's not the lack of family connections," his mother said. "I would hope you know us better than that. It's just that…oh, Reese, she's so young. And she comes from a world that's very different…"

"I already told you," Reese said tightly, "I can't be the father of Eliza's baby. I—"

"Enough!" Carlo made an angry gesture. "I will not tolerate lying. Ms. Mayhew is the daughter of a family friend as well as a classmate of your sister's. How could you be so careless?"

"Has she had a paternity test done?" Reese demanded. "Maybe you'd better think about who's being careless." He could feel his temper slipping the tight leash he'd held, and the words spilled out. Even the pain in his father's eyes couldn't halt his tongue. "Taking someone else's word without giving me a chance to defend myself? Fine." His eyes narrowed. "I don't need this, Dad. I'm not marrying Lying Eliza and you can't make me." He strode toward the door to the hallway.

"Don't you dare walk away when I'm speaking to you!" Reese had come by his temper honestly. Carlo stepped forward and reached for his son's arm, but Reese shoved him away in a red haze of anger.

"You ever put your hands on me again and I swear

you'll be sorry,'' he snarled at his father. He barreled down the hall to the heavy front door, oblivious to his mother's frantic cries. As he slammed through the door and the thunderous sound of its closing echoed behind him, he swore one thing to himself: he would never set foot in the same room with his father again until he'd received an apology from the old man.

Your opinion is important to us! Please take a few moments to share your thoughts with us about your experiences with Harlequin and Silhouette books. Your comments will be very useful in ensuring that we deliver books you love to read.

Please take a few minutes to complete the questionnaire, then send it to us at the address below.

Send your completed questionnaires to:
Harlequin/Silhouette Reader Survey, P.O. Box 9046, Buffalo, NY 14269-9046

1. As you may know, there are many different lines under the Harlequin and Silhouette brands. Each of the lines is listed below. Please check the box that most represents your reading habit for each line.

Line	Currently read this line	Do not read this line	Not sure if I read this line
Harlequin American Romance	❑	❑	❑
Harlequin Duets	❑	❑	❑
Harlequin Romance	❑	❑	❑
Harlequin Historicals	❑	❑	❑
Harlequin Superromance	❑	❑	❑
Harlequin Intrigue	❑	❑	❑
Harlequin Presents	❑	❑	❑
Harlequin Temptation	❑	❑	❑
Harlequin Blaze	❑	❑	❑
Silhouette Special Edition	❑	❑	❑
Silhouette Romance	❑	❑	❑
Silhouette Intimate Moments	❑	❑	❑
Silhouette Desire	❑	❑	❑

2. Which of the following best describes why you bought *this book?* One answer only, please.

- the picture on the cover ❑
- the author ❑
- part of a miniseries ❑
- saw an ad in a magazine/newsletter ❑
- I borrowed/was given this book ❑
- the title ❑
- the line is one I read often ❑
- saw an ad in another book ❑
- a friend told me about it ❑
- other: ______________ ❑

3. Where did you buy *this book?* One answer only, please.

- at Barnes & Noble ❑
- at Waldenbooks ❑
- at Borders ❑
- at another bookstore ❑
- at Wal-Mart ❑
- at Target ❑
- at Kmart ❑
- at another department store or mass merchandiser ❑
- at a grocery store ❑
- at a drugstore ❑
- on eHarlequin.com Web site ❑
- from another Web site ❑
- Harlequin/Silhouette Reader Service/through the mail ❑
- used books from anywhere ❑
- I borrowed/was given this book ❑

4. On average, how many Harlequin and Silhouette books do you buy at one time?

- I buy _______ books at one time ❑
- I rarely buy a book ❑

MRQ403SD-1A

5. How many times per month do you shop for any *Harlequin and/or Silhouette* books? One answer only, please.

1 or more times a week	❑	a few times per year	❑
1 to 3 times per month	❑	less often than once a year	❑
1 to 2 times every 3 months	❑	never	❑

6. When you think of your ideal heroine, which *one* statement describes her the best? One answer only, please.

She's a woman who is strong-willed	❑	She's a desirable woman	❑
She's a woman who is needed by others	❑	She's a powerful woman	❑
She's a woman who is taken care of	❑	She's a passionate woman	❑
She's an adventurous woman	❑	She's a sensitive woman	❑

7. The following statements describe types or genres of books that you may be interested in reading. Pick *up to 2 types* of books that you are most interested in.

I like to read about truly romantic relationships ❑
I like to read stories that are sexy romances ❑
I like to read romantic comedies ❑
I like to read a romantic mystery/suspense ❑
I like to read about romantic adventures ❑
I like to read romance stories that involve family ❑
I like to read about a romance in times or places that I have never seen ❑
Other: ______________________________ ❑

The following questions help us to group your answers with those readers who are similar to you. Your answers will remain confidential.

8. Please record your year of birth below.

19 ____

9. What is your marital status?

single ❑ married ❑ common-law ❑ widowed ❑
divorced/separated ❑

10. Do you have children 18 years of age or younger currently living at home?

yes ❑ no ❑

11. Which of the following best describes your employment status?

employed full-time or part-time ❑ homemaker ❑ student ❑
retired ❑ unemployed ❑

12. Do you have access to the Internet from either home or work?

yes ❑ no ❑

13. Have you ever visited eHarlequin.com?
yes ❑ no ❑

14. What state do you live in?

____

15. Are you a member of Harlequin/Silhouette Reader Service?

yes ❑ Account # ____________ no ❑ MRQ403SD-1B

HARLEQUIN BLAZE COVER MODEL SEARCH CONTEST 3569 OFFICIAL RULES
NO PURCHASE NECESSARY TO ENTER

1. To enter, submit two (2) 4" x 6" photographs of a boyfriend or spouse (who must be 18 years of age or older) taken no later than three (3) months from the time of entry: a close-up, waist up, shirtless photograph; and a fully clothed, full-length photograph, then, tell us, in 100 words or fewer, why he should be a Harlequin Blaze cover model and how he is romantic. Your complete "entry" must include: (i) your essay, (ii) the Official Entry Form and Publicity Release Form printed below completed and signed by you (as "Entrant"), (iii) the photographs (with your hand-written name, address and phone number, and your model's name, address and phone number on the back of each photograph), and (iv) the Publicity Release Form and Photograph Representation Form printed below completed and signed by your model (as "Model"), and should be sent via first-class mail to either: Harlequin Blaze Cover Model Search Contest 3569, P.O. Box 9069, Buffalo, NY, 14269-9069, or Harlequin Blaze Cover Model Search Contest 3569, P.O. Box 637, Fort Erie, Ontario L2A 5X3. All submissions must be in English and be received no later than September 30, 2003. Limit: one entry per person, household or organization. **Purchase or acceptance of a product offer does not improve your chances of winning.** All entry requirements must be strictly adhered to for eligibility and to ensure fairness among entries.

2. Ten (10) Finalist submissions (photographs and essays) will be selected by a panel of judges consisting of members of the Harlequin editorial, marketing and public relations staff, as well as a representative from Elite Model Management (Toronto) Inc., based on the following criteria:

Aptness/Appropriateness of submitted photographs for a Harlequin Blaze cover—70%
Originality of Essay—20%
Sincerity of Essay—10%

In the event of a tie, duplicate finalists will be selected. The photographs submitted by finalists will be posted on the Harlequin website no later than November 15, 2003 (at www.blazecovermodel.com), and viewers may vote, in rank order, on their favorite(s) to assist in the panel of judges' final determination of the Grand Prize and Runner-up winning entries based on the above judging criteria. All decisions of the judges are final.

3. All entries become the property of Harlequin Enterprises Ltd. and none will be returned. Any entry may be used for future promotional purposes. Elite Model Management (Toronto) Inc. and/or its partners, subsidiaries and affiliates operating as "Elite Model Management" will have access to all entries including all personal information, and may contact any Entrant and/or Model in its sole discretion for their own business purposes. Harlequin and Elite Model Management (Toronto) Inc. are separate entities with no legal association or partnership whatsoever having no power to bind or obligate the other or create any expressed or implied obligation or responsibility on behalf of the other, such that Harlequin shall not be responsible in any way for any acts or omissions of Elite Model Management (Toronto) Inc or its partners, subsidiaries and affiliates in connection with the Contest or otherwise and Elite Model Management shall not be responsible in any way for any acts or omissions of Harlequin or its partners, subsidiaries and affiliates in connection with the contest or otherwise.

4. All Entrants and Models must be residents of the U.S. or Canada, be 18 years of age or older, and have no prior criminal convictions. The contest is not open to any Model that is a professional model and/or actor in any capacity at the time of the entry. Contest void wherever prohibited by law; all applicable laws and regulations apply. Any litigation within the Province of Quebec regarding the conduct or organization of a publicity contest may be submitted to the Régie des alcools, des courses et des jeux for a ruling, and any litigation regarding the awarding of a prize may be submitted to the Régie only for the purpose of helping the parties reach a settlement. Employees and immediate family members of Harlequin Enterprises Ltd., D.L. Blair, Inc., Elite Model Management (Toronto) Inc. and their parents, affiliates, subsidiaries and all other agencies, entities and persons connected with the use, marketing or conduct of this Contest are not eligible to enter. Acceptance of any prize offered constitutes permission to use Entrants' and Models' names, essay submissions, photographs or other likenesses for the purposes of advertising, trade, publication and promotion on behalf of Harlequin Enterprises Ltd., its parent, affiliates, subsidiaries, assigns and other authorized entities involved in the judging and promotion of the contest without further compensation to any Entrant or Model, unless prohibited by law.

5. Finalists will be determined no later than October 30, 2003. Prize Winners will be determined no later than January 31, 2004. Grand Prize Winners (consisting of winning Entrant and Model) will be required to sign and return Affidavit of Eligibility/Release of Liability and Model Release forms within thirty (30) days of notification. Non-compliance with this requirement and within the specified time period will result in disqualification and an alternate will be selected. Any prize notification returned as undeliverable will result in the awarding of the prize to an alternate set of winners. All travelers (or parent/legal guardian of a minor) must execute the Affidavit of Eligibility/Release of Liability prior to ticketing and must possess required travel documents (e.g. valid photo ID) where applicable. Travel dates specified by Sponsor but no later than May 30, 2004.

6. Prizes: One (1) Grand Prize—the opportunity for the Model to appear on the cover of a paperback book from the Harlequin Blaze series, and a 3 day/2 night trip for two (Entrant and Model) to New York, NY for the photo shoot of Model which includes round-trip coach air transportation from the commercial airport nearest the winning Entrant's home to New York, NY, (or, in lieu of air transportation, $100 cash payable to Entrant and Model, if the winning Entrant's home is within 250 miles of New York, NY), hotel accommodations (double occupancy) at the Plaza Hotel and $500 cash spending money payable to Entrant and Model, (approximate prize value: $8,000), and one (1) Runner-up Prize of $200 cash payable to Entrant and Model for a romantic dinner for two (approximate prize value: $200). Prizes are valued in U.S. currency. Prizes consist of only those items listed as part of the prize. No substitution of prize(s) permitted by winners. All prizes are awarded jointly to the Entrant and Model of the winning entries, and are not severable - prizes and obligations may not be assigned or transferred. Any change to the Entrant and/or Model of the winning entries will result in disqualification and an alternate will be selected. Taxes on prize are the sole responsibility of winners. Any and all expenses and/or items not specifically described as part of the prize are the sole responsibility of winners. Harlequin Enterprises Ltd. and D.L. Blair, Inc., their parents, affiliates, and subsidiaries are not responsible for errors in printing of Contest entries and/or game pieces. No responsibility is assumed for lost, stolen, late, illegible, incomplete, inaccurate, non-delivered, postage due or misdirected mail or entries. In the event of printing or other errors which may result in unintended prize values or duplication of prizes, all affected game pieces or entries shall be null and void.

7. Winners will be notified by mail. For winners' list (available after March 31, 2004), send a self-addressed, stamped envelope to: Harlequin Blaze Cover Model Search Contest 3569 Winners, P.O. Box 4200, Blair, NE 68009-4200, or refer to the Harlequin website (at www.blazecovermodel.com).

Contest sponsored by Harlequin Enterprises Ltd., P.O. Box 9042, Buffalo, NY 14269-9042.

HBCVRMODEL2

COMING NEXT MONTH

#1537 MAN IN CONTROL—Diana Palmer
Long, Tall Texans
Undercover agent Alexander Cobb joined forces with his sworn enemy Jodie Clayburn to crack a case. Surprisingly, working together proved to be the easy part. The trouble they faced was fighting the fiery attraction that threatened to consume them both!

#1538 BORN TO BE WILD—Anne Marie Winston
Dynasties: The Barones
Celia Papleo had been just a girl when Reese Barone sailed out of her life, leaving her heart shattered. But now she was all woman—and more than a match for the wealthy man who tempted her again. Could a night of passion erase the misunderstandings of the past?

#1539 TEMPTING THE TYCOON—Cindy Gerard
Helping women find their happily-ever-afters was wedding planner Rachel Matthew's trade. But she refused to risk her own heart. That didn't stop roguishly charming millionaire lawyer Nate McGrory from wanting to claim her for himself…and envisioning her icy facade turing to molten lava at his touch!

#1540 LONETREE RANCHERS: MORGAN—Kathie DeNosky
Owning the most successful ranch in Wyoming was Morgan Wakefield's dream. And it was now within his grasp—as long as he wed Samantha Peterson. Their marriage was strictly a business arrangement—but it didn't stem the desire they felt when together….

#1541 HAVING THE BEST MAN'S BABY—Shawna Delacorte
For Jean Summerfield, the one thing worse than having to wear a bridesmaid dress was facing her unreliable ex, best man Ry Collier. But Jean's dormant desire sparked to life at Ry's touch. Would Ry stay to face the consequences of their passion, or leave her burned once more?

#1542 COWBOY'S MILLION-DOLLAR SECRET—Emilie Rose
Charismatic cowboy Patrick Lander knew exactly who he was—until virginal beauty Leanna Jensen brought news that Patrick would inherit his biological father's multimillion-dollar estate! The revelation threw Patrick's settled life into chaos—but paled compared to the emotions Leanna aroused in him.

SDCNM0903